Emako Blue

BRENDA WOODS

speak

An Imprint of Penguin Group (USA) Inc.

SPEAK

Published by the Penguin Group

Penguin Group (USA) Inc., 345 Hudson Street, New York, New York 10014, U.S.A.

Penguin Group (Canada), 90 Eglinton Avenue East, Suite 700, Toronto,
Ontario, Canada M4P 2Y3
(a division of Pearson Penguin Canada Inc.)

Penguin Books Ltd, 80 Strand, London WC2R 0RL, England

Penguin Ireland, 25 St Stephen's Green, Dublin 2, Ireland
(a division of Penguin Books Ltd)

Penguin Group (Australia), 250 Camberwell Road, Camberwell, Victoria 3124,
Australia (a division of Pearson Australia Group Pty Ltd)

Penguin Books India Pvt Ltd, 11 Community Centre, Panchsheel Park,
New Delhi - 110 017, India

Penguin Group (NZ), Cnr Airborne and Rosedale Roads, Albany, Auckland 1310,
New Zealand (a division of Pearson New Zealand Ltd)

Penguin Books (South Africa) (Pty) Ltd, 24 Sturdee Avenue,
Rosebank, Johannesburg 2196, South Africa

Registered Offices: Penguin Books Ltd, 80 Strand, London WC2R 0RL, England

First published in the United States of America by G. P. Putnam's Sons,
a division of Penguin Young Readers Group, 2004
Published by Speak, an imprint of Penguin Group (USA) Inc., 2005

Woods, 2004
ed

THE LIBRARY OF CONGRESS HAS CATALOGED THE PUTNAM EDITION AS FOLLOWS:
Woods, Brenda (Brenda A.) Emako Blue / by Brenda Woods. p.   cm.
Summary: Monterey, Savannah, Jamal, and Eddie have never had much to do with
each other until Emako Blue shows up at chorus practice, but just as the lives of the
five Los Angeles high school students become intertwined, tragedy tears them apart.
1. African Americans—Juvenile fiction. [1. African Americans—Fiction.
2. Interpersonal relations—Fiction. 3. High schools—Fiction. 4. Schools—Fiction.
5. Los Angeles—Fiction.]
I. Title.   PZ7.W86335Em 2004   [Fic]—dc22   2003016647
ISBN 0-399-24006-3

Speak ISBN 0-14-240418-7
Designed by Marikka Tamura
Text set in Caslon
Printed in the United States of America

To Lori Gonzalez

Acknowledgments

I thank God, who led me to and through this story. I also thank Barbara Markowitz for her continued support and kindness. Thank you to John Rudolph for his editorial skill and for sharing my vision. Finally, thank you to Nancy Paulsen and everyone at Putnam for allowing me the freedom to write about a difficult subject.
Life is precious.

Monterey

The parking lot at the church was full. A fat cop, parked on a motorcycle, waved us by with one hand while he wiped his forehead with the other. It was hot.

■ ■ ■

The air-conditioning in our Chevy Blazer was broken and my daddy's palms were so wet, he almost lost his grip on the steering wheel and cussed out loud. Mama dabbed at the back of her neck with a wrinkled white handkerchief. I was sweating too. No music played on the radio. Silence.

A crowd was standing in front of the church, but I knew that if Emako hadn't died the way she had, most of these people wouldn't be here. As for me, I belonged here. Emako was my *girl*.

Daddy found a parking space on the street and squeezed in between two cars. I slid out of the car and walked into the church, holding my mama and daddy's hands. I stood on my tiptoes, trying to see Emako's family, but there was a human shield around them all dressed in black.

I was wearing a short skirt, and when I sat down between my mama and daddy, the yellow wood of the pew felt cool against my bare brown legs.

"Today is a day of great sorrow!" the preacher's loud voice boomed, filling the church just as Eddie came and sat down in front of me. I touched him on the shoulder and he turned around. He looked into my eyes and squeezed my hand like he was trying to give me his strength. Tears started to roll down my cheeks and I let go of his hand and reached into my purse for a tissue.

"A sweet innocent life has been taken before her time!" the preacher shouted.

"Have mercy!" a woman in the front screamed.

"Amen!" a man yelled from the back of the church.

The choir director motioned to the choir with his hand and they stood up and began to hum and sway.

All of a sudden, Emako's mother, Verna, jumped up, stumbled over to the casket, and screamed, "Lord, no! Not my child!"

The choir stopped humming.

A man stood up, put his arm around her shoulders, and

took her back to her seat. My body started to tremble. Daddy hugged me and Mama took my hands. Silver stars and moons dangled from the bracelet that Emako had given me for my birthday.

"Who can comfort this mother? I ask, who?" the preacher shouted. "No one but the Lord!"

People all around me whispered, "Amen."

"Praise Jesus!" the preacher said softly. "Yet we have all come here today to try to comfort this mother, and this family, and to celebrate the short life of this young woman child, Emako Blue. We have come here today to try to make some sense out of this and we have come here today to say good-bye. But I say to each and every one of you, this is not really a good-bye, because Emako has just gone on ahead of us to a better place. And I say to this mother, you will see your child again on the other side, in that place we call Paradise."

I wanted to tell him to stop, but the preacher was going on and on and his words were loud and hard, like cymbals banging.

Tragedy! Outrage! Atrocity!

Then softer words, like a violin.

Sweetness. Innocence. Like a lamb.

The choir stood and filled the church with a song called "Bringing in the Sheaves," and I hesitated before I stood up to take my place in the procession of mourners at the front of the church, mostly because I wanted to remember Emako the way she was. My legs got weak and my daddy put his arms around me and held me up.

I turned my head and saw Emako's mama. I swallowed hard as I started to cry again, but I was careful not to let her see the tears as the beginning of another salty stream touched my upper lip.

I walked slowly toward the coffin and stared. Emako. My *girl*. Emako Blue. She looked beautiful and her casket was baby pink.

Daddy led me back to the pew and we sat down. The church was finally quiet.

I put my head on my daddy's shoulder.

I remembered the first time I met Emako.

My mind left the church.

■ ■ ■

It was the beginning of the school year. I was a sophomore and I was trying out for the school chorus, waiting in the auditorium for my turn to sing. There were twenty of us trying out for twelve spots. Mr. Santos, the director of the chorus, sat at the piano, warming up, and everyone was talking, filling the room with noise.

Mr. Santos stopped playing the piano, looked at a sheet of paper, and called a name. "Sage Hudson."

A white girl with pale pink skin and long curly red hair walked up the steps and I could tell she was scared. She had a high voice that made most people in the room shut up and I imagined her singing music like opera or something. I wondered if my voice was good enough and part of me wanted to get up and leave.

Mr. Santos looked at his list again. "Savannah Parker." This light-skinned black girl with a really big butt ran up the steps and almost tripped and fell. She was short but she was wearing shoes with four-inch heels. She had a good voice but she sang a little off-key. I took a deep breath and decided to stay. Maybe I had a chance.

"Could we have some quiet?" Mr. Santos asked.

We kept talking.

Mr. Santos shook his head and looked at his list. "Emako Blue."

She stood up, and as she walked up the steps, she immediately had the attention of all of the fellas in the room.

"Damn! She's fine!" I heard one of them say.

Then she opened her mouth and her voice poured out into the auditorium. It was like vanilla incense, smoky and sweet.

She had a voice that could do tricks, go high, low, and anywhere in between: a voice that's a gift from God. She was Jill Scott and Minnie Riperton, Lauryn Hill and India.Arie.

She was way too pretty, with dark brown skin and black braids extended to her waist.

She was wearing tight faded blue jeans, a red sleeveless T-shirt, and black platform shoes. She was kind of tall, with a tight body like a video freak. I could feel jealousy and lust creeping around the room, and when she finished singing, the room was as quiet as a library at midnight.

Everyone in the audience clapped. Mr. Santos stood up and clapped too. He acted like he had found a star.

Jamal, this fine brother who was sitting behind me, asked the guy who was sitting next to him, "Hey, Eddie, is she beautiful or what?"

"She's beautiful," Eddie replied.

"I'm gonna havta get with that," Jamal said.

Eddie just laughed. "Player, you crazy."

Emako walked down the steps and sat down in the empty seat next to me. I smiled at her and she smiled back. Her teeth were perfect and white. I ran my tongue over my braces. She wore silver rings on every finger, including her thumbs, and had a tattoo of a small red rose on her right shoulder. Confidence was all around her and I took some of it with me when Mr. Santos called my name next.

I walked up the steps slowly, cleared my throat three times, and sang a song called "Santa Baby" that Eartha Kitt had made famous. It was a song my mama always played at Christmastime, a song I knew all the words to. When I finished, a few people clapped and Mr. Santos gave me a thumbs-up. I made it, I thought. I laughed out loud and returned to my seat.

"You can sing," Emako said.

I thought she was just messing with me. "Yeah, right."

"No, for real. What's your name?"

"Monterey," I replied.

"My name's Emako. Holler at you t'morrow," she said as she walked out of the auditorium into the sun.

I looked at my watch. It was almost four-thirty. I picked up my backpack and left like a deer, quietly.

I went outside and sat down under a tree on a low brick wall in front of the school, waiting for my daddy to pick me up. Cars rolled by and a warm breeze blew. It was a perfect day in L.A. I put on my sunglasses to keep from squinting into the sun.

I thought about Emako and wondered why I had never seen her before and why she would even talk to me. Girls like her hardly ever did. They usually acted like I wasn't around, like I was invisible, like I was a nobody. My best friend, Simone, had moved away over the summer and I felt kind of lonely. I took a deep breath and looked at my watch.

"Sorry I'm late," he said as I climbed into the car.

"You're always late," I replied, and turned on the radio. "I could always take the bus, you know," I added. "I'm not a little girl anymore."

"You're the only little girl I have and I don't want you taking the bus. It's not safe."

"Nothing's gonna happen to me. You worry too much, Daddy."

"Monterey?"

"Yes?"

"Didn't we just talk about this yesterday?"

"Yes," I replied.

"Let's just say that I don't want to talk about it again, okay?"

"Okay," I mumbled. "I made it into chorus," I added.

"That's sensational. My little girl can sing," he said with a smile.

Little girl. Those words made me want to scream, but instead I just turned up the radio and looked out of the window, hoping I would get home in time to watch *106 & Park*.

We got home just as it started. I hurried to my room, locked the door, and turned on the TV.

I had only been home for about five minutes when I heard my mama open the garage door to come into the house. She knocked on my door. "Monterey?"

"Yeah?"

"How was school?" She asked the same question every day.

I gave the same answer every day: "Fine."

She tried the doorknob. "Why's the door locked? Haven't I told you not to lock your door?"

"I'm not a baby anymore. I'm fifteen and it's my room."

"Monterey, are you tryin' to get fresh with me? Open this door."

I opened the door partway and peeked. "I made it into chorus."

"My baby can sing! It's what I tell everyone. I say, my baby can sing!" She hugged me tight.

I squirmed. "Mama, it's just the chorus."

"I know. But still. I'm so happy for you," she said as she released me.

"Thanks," I said, and closed the door. I locked it quietly, waiting for her to say something, but she didn't.

I could hear one of her old-school CDs playing while she was cooking.

Daddy was outside watering *his* grass.

I stayed in my room until dinner was ready.

■ ■ ■

I didn't see Emako again until the first day of chorus practice.

"Monterey?" Mr. Santos said. "I want you in the second row, next to Emako."

"Okay," I responded. Great, I thought. Now no one will hear my voice.

"Hey, Monterey," Emako said as I squeezed in between her and that girl with the big butt, Savannah.

"Hey, Emako."

I looked at Savannah. "Hey," I said, but she turned her head and looked away. I started to feel invisible.

Emako saw what Savannah did and whispered, "What's up with bubble butt?"

I giggled and shrugged my shoulders.

"Question number one: Are we here to sing or to talk?" Mr. Santos asked.

"We are here to sing," a boy in the row behind me said loudly.

"Thank you, Mr. Eddie Ortiz, star tenor," Mr. Santos replied.

"De nada," Eddie said, and took a bow.

I turned around and glanced at Eddie. He was Hispanic, with dark hair and green eyes. He smiled at me. I got nervous and started to bite my nails.

"Hi," he said.

I couldn't speak. I turned back to the front of the room. He is too cute, I thought.

Mr. Santos sat down at the piano. "Middle C. The most important note in music. Who can give me a middle C? Jamal?"

"Why you gotta pick on me the first day?" Jamal shook his head.

"Would you prefer that I wait until next week?" Mr. Santos asked.

"No," Jamal responded, "I prefer that you wait until next year."

10

Eddie was standing next to Jamal. "You a crazy fool," he said loud enough for everyone to hear.

"Why you wanna disrespect me like that, Eddie? You spozed to be my dawg."

"Okay, let's settle down," Mr. Santos said.

All we sang for one whole hour were scales and I started to wonder when this was going to start to be fun.

Finally, practice was over.

Jamal touched Emako on the shoulder and said, "Let me talk to you a minute."

"About what?" Emako replied.

"About me and you."

Savannah whipped around to stare at Jamal.

Jamal stared back. "You got somethin' to say?"

"Player!" Savannah said. "Gina is my best friend."

"Gina don't own me!"

"I don't have time for no nonsense," Emako said. "Y'all 'bout to make me miss my bus." Emako walked away and I trailed along after her. She walked fast.

Emako saw her bus and started to run, but it left before she could get to it. "Now I gotta wait another hour, and my mama gotta get to work, and I'm spozed to be home by four-thirty cuz I gotta watch my little brother and sister, and now she's gonna get all upset and try to make me quit the chorus."

"I could ask my mama to give you a ride if you want me to," I said. "Usually my daddy picks me up, but he's at home becuz he fell down the steps and twisted his ankle. It turned all black and blue and he's walking with crutches, but he still can't go to work or drive the car." I checked my watch. It was three forty-five. "She should be here at four. She's always on time. Not like my daddy. He's always late."

Emako gave me a look like I was talking too much. "You sure? Cuz I don't live around here."

"I'm sure."

We sat down together and waited.

"Did you go here last year? Becuz I don't remember you."

"No, I transferred from Truman."

"In South Central?"

"Yeah." She paused. "But I like it better here . . . on the Westside."

"You live in South Central?"

"Always have. You live around here, huh?" she asked.

"Yeah."

"I figured."

"Why you gotta say that?" I asked.

"I mean you just seem like you live on a nice little street with trees and all that, where nuthin' real bad ever happens and you probably got a collection of Barbie dolls, PlayStation One and Two, your own DVD player, and a little pink bedroom."

"I'm not rich or nuthin'."

She was getting ready to say something when Mama honked the horn. I opened the car door and stuck my head in. "This is Emako and she needs a ride home becuz she missed her bus and she has to be home by four-thirty to baby-sit. I told her it would be okay. Okay?"

"Okay. Hi, Emako."

"Hi, Miz . . ."

"Hamilton," I said.

"Hi, Miz Hamilton," Emako said, and climbed into the backseat.

"Where do you live, Emako?"

"Near Ninety-fifth Street and Dover."

"Four o'clock," Mama said. "We should be able to make it in time."

"Thank you, Miz Hamilton," Emako said.

"DeeDee, call me DeeDee," Mama said, and put her foot on the gas.

Mama drove too fast. She always drove too fast. We rounded the corner and the tires screeched.

"Emako . . . isn't that a Japanese name?" Mama asked.

"Yes," Emako replied.

"What's your last name, Emako?"

"Blue . . . Emako Blue."

"What a beautiful name," Mama said.

"Thank you," Emako replied.

Oh, no, Mama's going to keep talking, I thought. I

turned on the radio to her oldies station and she started to hum. I took a deep breath and rolled down the window.

It seemed like magic as we made almost every green light and soon we were on Emako's street.

"It's the house on the corner," Emako said.

It was a tiny yellow house with grass that needed cutting. We pulled up to the curb and Mama stopped the car.

"Thanks, Miz Hamilton."

"DeeDee," Mama reminded her.

"Thanks, DeeDee," Emako said as she got out. "Later, Monterey."

"Later, Emako."

She waved at me from the front door and disappeared inside.

"She seems nice," Mama said as we sped away.

"Yeah, she's cool," I replied. "Real cool."

■ ■ ■

The next day I saw Emako at her locker.

"Monterey is just too much name for one person," Emako said. She threw her books into her locker and slammed it shut.

"My little cousin tried to start callin' me Rey, but my mama said that if she had wanted people to call me Rey, she woulda named me Rey," I replied as we headed to chorus practice. "Why'd your mama name you Emako? You ain't Japanese," I said.

"Sure I am," she replied.

"Sure you are what?"

"Japanese."

"You don't look Japanese."

She laughed loudly and pointed her finger in my face. "You are too square, Monterey."

"Come on, be serious," I insisted.

"Okay. My mama used to know this Japanese nurse at County Hospital, where she worked before I was born. Her name was Emako and Mama liked her. She said she was real sweet. So Mama named me after her."

"I got named Monterey becuz my mama got pregnant with me at the Monterey Jazz Festival. Maybe that's why I like to sing." I crossed my eyes.

Emako laughed again.

A tall, smooth, dark senior with a shaved head who played football and called himself Reggie H passed us in the hall. "Hey, Miss Emako."

"Hey, Reggie." Emako smiled at him like they had a secret. They watched each other walk away in opposite directions.

"You know him?" I asked.

"Yeah. My older brother Dante used to play Pop Warner football with him."

"You been with him?"

"I ain't been with nobody, yet."

"Me neither."

We entered the auditorium just as Mr. Santos started handing out sheet music. We were learning to read music.

Emako whispered into my ear, "This is wastin' my time. All I gotta do is hear the music once, maybe twice, and I remember the melody. Sometimes I can pick up the harmony."

I looked down at the sheet music, and as I took my place, I bumped right into Eddie. The skin on his face was tan. "Excuse me, Monterey," he said.

"Hey, Eddie," I said, trying to keep my mouth closed so that he wouldn't see my braces. I took a deep breath. Eddie smiled and took his position behind me.

Emako whispered into my ear, "You like him, huh?"

"Like who?" I asked.

"Eddie."

"He's okay."

"His eyes are pretty," Emako said.

"For real," I replied.

Mr. Santos looked at us and cleared his throat.

"Are we here to talk or to sing, Monterey?" Mr. Santos asked.

"To sing."

Mr. Santos began to play the scales and our voices echoed them back.

After practice I asked Emako, "You wanna go to Knott's

Berry Farm for this Halloween thing on Saturday with me and my baby cousin Lynette?"

She looked at me like I had lost my mind. "Let me guess. Your daddy 'n' mama gonna drive us there and pick us up b'fore midnight like three little Cinderellas? Naw. Sorry. B'sides, I gotta watch my brother and sister till my mama gets home. She gotta work a double shift."

"You lyin', Emako."

"Why you wanna think that, Monterey?" She was wearing orange lip gloss and she smiled without showing any teeth, looking like a brown Mona Lisa.

We went outside to the bus stop.

"I mean, all you havta say is I don't wanna go," I said.

"Okay, I don't wanna go."

"Why? Becuz you too grown?"

"Yeah, I'm too grown."

"You too grown to hang with me?"

"Don't get all mad. It just ain't my thing. But you and your little cousin have fun," she said as she climbed the steps onto the bus.

The bus doors closed and it sped away, leaving a trail of dust and fumes.

■ ■ ■

My phone was ringing when I got home. I made a dive for the bed and picked it up before the fourth ring. "Hello?"

"Hey." It was Emako. She'd never called me before.

"Hey, Emako." I tried to say it without feeling.

"You mad, huh?"

"I ain't mad," I lied.

"You wanna come to my house on Sunday?" she asked. "I gotta sing in the choir at church in the morning, but I get home about twelve-thirty."

"Oh, now you wanna be nice."

"You wanna come or not?"

■ ■ ■

That Sunday my daddy raised his eyebrows when we turned onto Figueroa. South Central. He had grown up here, but he didn't like to drive through these streets. When he pulled to a stop at a red light, he checked the doors to make sure they were locked.

A black man crossed the street with two muzzled pit bulls on short leashes.

On one corner there was a motel painted lime green with red doors.

The neon sign blinked.

Vacancy.

He parked the car in front of Emako's house and ushered me to the door like I was in the fifth grade.

"I'm fifteen, Daddy," I said.

"Precisely."

"I'm not a baby."

"That's what you want to believe. You will always be my

baby." He rang the doorbell. It didn't work. He knocked on the rusty white security door.

"It's open," said a little girl's voice from the other side.

Daddy was reaching for the door when I heard Emako's voice. "Just a minute." The door opened and Emako smiled.

"Hey, Monterey."

"Hey, Emako," I said, and smiled back.

My daddy extended his hand as he followed me into the house. "I'm Monterey's daddy, Mr. Hamilton."

Emako shook his hand. The door closed behind us.

Emako's mother was sitting in an orange vinyl chair too close to the television, wearing a white slip, sipping ice water from a jelly jar. When she saw my daddy, she put down her water, stood up, wiped her damp hand on her slip, and reached for my daddy's hand.

"Verna Blue," she introduced herself, holding his hand a little too long.

"Roman Hamilton . . . ," Daddy said, releasing her hand.

Verna looked me over and said, "You must be Monterey."

"Yes, Mrs. Blue," I replied politely.

"No Mrs., just Verna. Gotta have a Mr. to be a Mrs. and I haven't had no Mr. in a while." She glanced at my daddy in a funny way.

Emako's seven-year-old sister, Latrice, ran out the front door, eating a thick slice of ham.

"Latrice! Get your butt back in this house! What'd I tell you?" Verna raised her voice.

Latrice stepped back into the house. " 'Bout what?"

" 'Bout eatin' outside like you ain't got no table to sit down to."

Latrice went over to the table with a mouthful of ham and sat down. "And chew with your mouth closed," Verna added.

"Yeah," Marcel, Emako's nine-year-old brother, yelled from the other room.

Emako looked down like she felt ashamed.

"I'll pick you up at seven, Monterey," Daddy said as he backed out the door. Something told me that he couldn't wait to get away from the streets he had once called home. Emako and I followed him outside and stood on the porch.

We watched him turn the corner just as a Regal with tinted windows rolled by slowly, like a hearse. The window was down and a fine caramel-colored brother wearing a black bandana and two gold watches on his left wrist called out to Emako. "What up, baby girl?"

Emako tilted her head to the side. The caramel-colored brother grinned as he drove down the middle of the street, leaving a trail of music behind him.

"Who's that?" I asked.

"No one," she replied.

"He's fine."

"Just got outta CYA . . . California Youth Authority. Like jail." Emako talked to me like she was giving me an education.

"I know what CYA is," I replied. "Why you gotta talk to me like I'm a child?"

"Just checking. I just don't want you to get caught up with no gangbanger. You ain't about that. That's part of why I transferred away from Truman. To try to get away from all that. Too much trouble in the classrooms and everywhere else."

"Were you scared?"

"I ain't scared of nuthin', but I got tired of all the non-sense. Every day it was somethin'. School police everywhere. Some brotha all up on me. Some little sista and her clique all in my face becuz her little dude's tryin' to get with me. And I wasn't thinking 'bout none of 'em. You understand what I'm sayin'?"

"I understand."

We went back inside and Emako locked the door like she was locking out the world. Verna turned up the TV. Emako and I went into the bedroom she shared with Latrice and turned on her PlayStation. Marcel stuck his head in the door.

Emako looked up. "Get outta here b'fore I kick your little butt."

"Mama! Emako said she's gonna kick my butt!"

Verna answered from the living room. "Marcel! Leave them girls alone. Can't y'all give me some peace?"

Marcel stuck out his tongue before he disappeared from the hallway. Emako put on a Mary J. Blige CD and we started to sing along.

After a while Emako stopped singing and said, "I'll be as big as her . . . you watch. . . . I'll be livin' it up. I'll move my mama away from all this madness and buy her a house with a pool in Malibu that looks out over the ocean, send my little brother and sister to private school in a limo . . . ," she said, and paused. "You can sing backup while you watch my back."

"I'm gonna watch your back? You got it all figured out."

"Yeah, cuz you got a good heart."

"My mama and daddy want me to go to college, be a veterinarian or something."

"That what you wanna be, a doggie doctor? I thought you wanted to do the music thing."

"I dunno. I like animals."

"Sometimes I think about that," Emako said.

"About bein' a doggie doctor?" I asked.

"No, about goin' to college."

"To be what?"

"I dunno . . . somethin'. But then I figure God gave me this talent so I could get up outta here."

Emako reached for the CD player, turned up the volume, and the music took over the tiny room.

For lunch we had ham sandwiches on white bread and 7 UP. Verna watched cable all day. Marcel poked his head in once in a while, getting the same reaction from Emako every time. Latrice spent the afternoon next door.

Everything was cool.

Jamal

I walked through the doors of the church behind Monterey, but she was so messed up that I don't think she even noticed me. Monterey and Emako were tight—different, but tight. You know . . . like opposite sides of the same coin. I decided not to speak to her. I didn't know what to say anyway.

I slid into a pew and spotted Eddie. He nodded and looked away.

I hung my head, trying to find some more tears, but they were all gone. I had cried almost without stopping for three nights straight.

I wanted to scream.

I wanted to break some heads.

I wanted to get the MF who had done this.

But I couldn't.

I had to leave it to the police or God.

I looked up as the preacher spoke from the pulpit. " 'Vengeance is mine; I will repay,' saith the Lord." It was like he was reading my mind.

■ ■ ■

Most people don't know this, but the first time I ever met Emako, she was in the fifth grade. She was this real cute little skinny girl. We were both taking piano lessons from this born-again Christian piano teacher who always said praise the Lord when you walked through the door. Her house always smelled like fried chicken or collard greens, and as soon as I sat down, my mouth would begin to water and all I could think about was my next meal.

My moms was making me take lessons, saying musical talent ran in the family from way back, but I didn't want the fellas to know because then they would have started to get in my face. So, I kept it quiet.

Emako was ahead of me and the teacher would get mad at her because Emako didn't want to learn to read music. Emako had told her that all she had to do was watch and listen, like she was some kind of musical genius. I guess the born-again music teacher wasn't interested in genius because one day Emako wasn't there and I never saw her again until that day in September when she showed up for chorus. I almost didn't recognize her. She sure wasn't a skinny little girl anymore, and when she opened her mouth to sing, I thought to myself, the born-again lady should be here now. Emako had become a mellow songstress with perfect pitch, and her body was bangin'.

I could see it all. I would write the music and produce the tracks. We would be kickin' it all over the world, concerts, BET, the Grammy Awards, MTV, music videos.

I stared at her hard, trying to make eye contact, but she didn't seem to see me. I wanted to hand her a bouquet of lavender roses and tell her she had my heart. Crazy love.

When class was over, I was just about to make my move when Savannah interrupted, starting some mess about Gina, and by the time I got Savannah to shut her mouth, Emako was gone. So I just went out to the parking lot, got in my ride, opened the sunroof, and drove off.

I was thinking about Emako's pretty mouth and little tiny waist when Gina popped back into my mind. Gina was sort of my girlfriend, a girl my moms had introduced me to. She was the daughter of one of the judges that Moms knew from the courthouse, where she worked as a court reporter.

Gina was kinda fly, and once, when her parents were in Las Vegas, she invited me over and we did the thing and now it was like she had a short leash around my neck. She wore honey-colored contact lenses and went to this private girl's school. I liked Gina, but it wasn't like I was loving her or anything.

When I got home, I opened the front door and called out to my moms but got no answer.

I changed into a tank top and shorts, and went out to the backyard. I dribbled the ball a little, then turned and shot. The ball made the sweetest sound as it slipped into the net and bounced back to me. I thought about Emako and grinned. Yeah, it was destiny.

■ ■ ■

A couple of days passed before I had the chance to get her alone without Gina's little watchdog Savannah being on my case. It had just started raining as school let out and I saw her waiting for the bus. I took a deep breath and slipped into player mode.

I touched her on the arm and she turned around.

"You remember me . . . from piano lessons?" I asked.

She looked at me hard like she was trying to remember my face. Then the look changed and she smiled. "Praise the Lord!"

I smiled back. "I could give you a ride home."

"Cool," she replied.

This was going to be easier than I thought.

I opened the door for her and she slid into my ride. "Thanks." She reminded me of chocolate syrup. Brown, sweet, and smooth.

There was heat trapped inside the car and it warmed me as I turned the key. I put in an Aaliyah CD.

"Aaliyah . . . she was too sweet." She turned up the volume.

I turned on the windshield wipers and made my way out of the parking lot onto the street.

The weather had driven most folks inside, but on some corners men stood selling oversized black-and-white umbrellas, taking advantage of the rain.

"You wanna stop at McDonald's?" I asked.

"Okay," she replied.

We picked up some food at the drive-thru and drove to her house. We stayed in the car, eating double cheeseburgers and french fries, and sharing ketchup.

"You got a boyfriend?" I finally asked.

"I got a few that like to come around, but they ain't about nuthin'. You know. Immature."

"So you're looking for a mature brother?"

"That's right. I'm tired of all this juvenile nonsense."

"What you think about me?"

"You're a'ight," Emako said, and looked at her watch.

"Just a'ight?"

She took a sip of orange soda and I was just getting ready to make a move when she opened the door and got out. "I gotta go. My mama has to go to work. Thanks, Jamal. Peace."

I lowered my voice. "Yeah, peace."

I drove away slowly, watching her in the rearview mirror as she walked up the short path to her house, because baby girl was so fine.

Gina was cool, but Emako was mo' better.

Savannah

Monterey entered the church and glared at me like I didn't belong there. I said to myself, No, she did not disrespect me up in here. But you know what? I didn't let it bother me. I mean, we all had the right to say good-bye to Emako, even me.

I know that most people thought that I was hating on Emako or something, and I suppose I was, but you gotta understand. I mean, the girl had everything going for her. She could sing. And, yeah, she was pretty. I had to give her that too. But she was . . . nice. That was the part that really messed with me. That was the part I didn't trust. I thought she was just acting and I was waiting for her mask to come off so that I could see what was underneath.

Now, if Emako had been like me, we would have been too tight. But no matter what I did to that girl, she wouldn't let me pull her down into my little hell. That's too deep, huh?

I looked around the church. I was sorry. But now I would never be able to tell her that. So, I suppose Emako had won the battle. The war had started at the beginning of the year.

■ ■ ■

By October, I was already wishing the year were over. I was too tired of getting up at 6:30, five days a week. School sucked.

Emako was talking to Mr. Santos when I showed up at chorus that day and Jamal was staring at her like he'd been hypnotized. Again. Jamal was trying to be a player, but I was keeping an eye on him because his girlfriend, Gina, was my best friend. Gina and I lived in the same neighborhood and we had gone to the same private school before they kicked me out because I failed geometry and refused to go to summer school. What did I look like, a mathematician?

I went over to where he was standing and got in his face.

"Why you always trippin', Savannah?" he said.

"Because Gina is my girl and I'm sure she would like to know that you are in here tryin' to get in ghetto girl's face. I mean, do I look like I'm blind?"

"No, it just looks like you're ugly!" Jamal raised his voice.

"Get outta my face. I don't know why Gina wants to be with you anyway. You ain't even on her level."

"But I'm fine."

I sneered at him. "Shut up."

"Thought so," Jamal said, having the last word.

Eddie started to laugh.

"What you laughin' at, Eddie? You ain't even in this," I said.

Before Eddie could say anything, Mr. Santos got out his tuning forks and told us to be quiet. I thought to myself, What kind of a name is that for a sister, Emako? Like having a Japanese name was going to stop her from being ghetto.

Emako began to sing and took over the room with that voice. I looked her over from head to toe. I thought about the house in the hills with the view of the city and the swimming pool that I went home to every day, and that made me feel good, like I had something that she didn't.

After an hour of the Emako show, previously called chorus, I went outside and waited for my mother. She pulled up in her new white Mercedes and I got in.

"How was school?" she asked.

"Same as every day, boring," I replied.

I switched the channel on the radio to 100.3, The Beat, and pumped up the volume.

"Turn that ghetto music down," my mother said.

"It's not ghetto music. Everyone listens to it, even white kids."

"Even white kids. That makes it okay?"

"That's not what I meant. Why is everyone on my case today? Could you just get off my back! Turn on whatever you want or just turn it off! Whatever!"

"Why are you so upset? I just asked you to turn the music down," she asked.

I turned off the radio. "Just leave me alone."

My mother took a deep breath and sighed.

We drove the rest of the way in silence.

When we got home, my mother's silky terrier, Lillie, met us at the front door, yelping. My mother picked her up in her arms and kissed her. Sometimes I think my mother loves that little dog more than she loves me. I hated that dog.

I went to my room and sat down to check my e-mail. I looked down at the ring on my pinkie finger that had a real diamond, not a cubic z, then looked at myself in the mirror. I thought about Emako and decided to start a little something.

■ ■ ■

I thought I would have to wait awhile for the perfect opportunity, but I didn't. The next day before lunch, I went into the bathroom and there she was. Alone.

"Hey, Emako," I said as the door closed behind me.

Emako was standing in front of the mirror, putting on lip gloss. She turned and smiled. "Hey, Savannah."

I walked over to the mirror and stood beside her. I stared into the mirror at her reflection. "I need to talk to you," I said.

"About what?" she asked.

"About Jamal."

"What about him?"

"His girlfriend, Gina, is my best friend. We used to go to the Cartwright School together. Have you ever heard of that school?"

"Not really," Emako replied.

"It's in Beverly Hills."

"Oh."

"Gina's father is a judge."

"What's that got to do with Jamal?"

"I see him tryin' to be all up on you. But I suppose you're used to that."

"Ain't nuthin'."

"Anyway, Jamal and Gina been together for two years. Real tight. And sometimes Jamal tries to be a player. But he always gets back with Gina when he's finished with his little chicken heads."

"I'm not a little chicken head."

"I know that, and that's why I wanted to let you know.

So you won't get your feelings hurt. I'm just tryin' to be nice." I gave her my most sincere look, hoping she would swallow it.

Emako turned away from the mirror and looked me in the face. "I'll remember that."

Eddie

When I got to the church, I started looking for the holy water. Then I remembered that it wasn't a Catholic church. I made the sign of the cross anyway.

There were plenty of people everywhere and by the time I found a seat, the minister had already started talking. Someone put a hand on my shoulder and I turned around and stared into Monterey's bloodshot eyes. She squeezed my hand and I watched the tears roll down her cheeks, but I kept my tears. I stayed strong. Strong.

I let go of her and looked forward, listening to the minister's words. Sobs and moans were coming from everywhere. Sorrow floated through the air.

I pictured Emako with angel's wings, flying through the

church like she was happy. I know it wasn't right, but I started to smile. You have to understand. She sang like a *pájarito*, like a bird.

■ ■ ■

I had been in the chorus last year. We'd do these concerts at Christmas, and Mr. Santos was teaching us to read music. He was cool and I liked to sing. Besides, I thought it would look good on my transcripts.

The first time I saw Emako, I thought she looked good, but I was always shy around girls like her.

The one I really wanted to talk to was her friend Monterey. I thought she was cute, but every time I said something to her, she acted nervous.

One day I tried to talk to Monterey after practice. She was standing beside Emako.

"Hey, Eddie," Emako said.

"Hey," I replied.

Monterey grinned at me without showing her braces, but she didn't say anything, so I said to Emako, "You have a fantastic voice."

"Thanks," was her reply. She gave me a funny look and I hoped she didn't think I was trying to come on to her.

Monterey just stared at me.

"And you too, Monterey. You have a good voice too," I added.

Monterey remained silent.

"See ya," I said, and turned to go.

"Peace," was their reply.

I caught my bus just as it was pulling away from the curb, and sat down for the long ride home. I thought about Monterey and wondered if she would ever talk to me. She seemed even more shy than me. Maybe I should ask her for her phone number. What if she said no?

I shook my head. I had more important things to think about. It was my senior year and I couldn't wait to graduate. I had gone to summer school three years in a row to graduate early.

I couldn't wait for my future to become my present, for the present to become my past.

I couldn't wait to be in college and away from the streets that had taught me to watch my back, day and night, the streets that had caught my only brother, Tomas.

Tomas.

He was incarcerated.

His body was covered with jailhouse tats.

Me, I was clean, the joy of my mother, my father's hope.

The bus came to a stop and some loud kids from middle school stumbled down the aisle and sat down. I gazed out of the window as the bus began to crawl through streets cluttered with cars, horns honking, women holding the hands of children who could barely walk, pulling them across the streets, lights turning red, orange hands flashing DON'T WALK, sidewalks buckled, gray concrete pushed up by the roots of rebellious trees. An ambulance screamed by and the bus stopped. I thought about Monterey again and smiled because she was kind of shy, like me. Then a car backfired and I jumped. L.A. was making me nervous.

"Hortensia?" I called when I got in the house.

"What?" my baby sister yelled from her room.

"Just checking," I said.

She peeked through her door. She was little and pretty, like my mother. "Checking what?"

"To make sure you're okay," I replied.

"You worry too much. Like it's your job to worry. You need to get a new job."

"Shut up. You're only saying that because you heard Mom say it," I said.

"It's true," she said, and closed the door to her room.

I looked in the refrigerator. "You want something to eat?" I yelled.

"No!"

I glanced up at the clock. My mother will walk through the door any minute, I thought, and then she will wash her hands and start to cook. The house will start to smell good.

I closed the refrigerator and checked the mail. There was another letter from Tomas. That meant tonight my mother would read it and cry. I took the letter into my room and put it in a drawer. I didn't want her to see it. I was getting tired of her tears for Tomas.

Monterey

Emako and I were getting tighter and tighter. At least once a week she was at my house or I was at hers, and we always ate lunch together.

The day before Thanksgiving, I was standing at my locker when Emako grabbed my arm.

"You comin' with me!" she said. It was a statement, not a question.

"Where?"

"To Melrose."

"On the bus?"

"Yeah, on the bus."

"I havta call my daddy," I said, loading my backpack with books.

"I'll be outside," she said, and began to walk away. She stopped and turned around. "It's vacation, Monterey. What's with all the books?"

"I gotta study."

"Ain't it a shame," she said, waving her empty backpack.

I stopped at the pay phone and called my daddy to tell him, really to ask him.

"Yes, I have enough money for a taxi if it gets too dark. . . . Yes, it would be a good idea if I had my own cell phone for emergencies. . . . Yes, I remembered to bring home my books to study." He was getting on my nerves.

We got off the bus and strolled down Melrose, passing shops where they sell see-through bell-bottoms and thong bikinis, and my eyes were wide open like a tourist's. A transvestite passed us wearing six-inch silver heels, a skintight lime-green spandex dress, a waist-length red wig, and rhinestone earrings. We laughed ourselves into a small jewelry shop.

I picked up a bracelet with little dangling moons and stars. "This is dope, huh?"

"Yeah, it's kinda sweet," Emako said, looking at the tiny price tag. "Thirty-five dollars," she said, squinting.

I put down the bracelet, opened my wallet, and counted my money. "I only have twenty dollars," I said.

Emako counted her money. "I only have nine dollars."

I looked at the bracelet once more. "Maybe it'll still be here the next time we come."

"Yeah, maybe," she replied.

We went back onto the street just as two tattooed men went by, both wearing leather vests and spiked blue hair.

"Freaky, huh?" Emako said.

"Yeah," I replied.

We kept going down Melrose until Emako stopped in front of Johnny Rockets. "You ever eat in there?" Emako asked.

"No," I replied. "You?"

"No," she answered. "You hungry?"

I looked at her and smiled. "Yeah."

We strutted in, sat down in a window booth, and I felt like I was grown.

■ ■ ■

That Saturday, Emako and I were sitting in my room, listening to CDs.

My daddy knocked on the door. "What kind of pizza do you kids want?"

I looked over at Emako, who shrugged her shoulders.

I replied, "Thin crust, pepperoni and sausage, no tomatoes, and some Mountain Dew . . . and we're not kids, Daddy," I added.

"Sorry," he said through the cracked-open door.

Emako picked up a copy of *Vibe* magazine. She held it up in front of me and pointed to a picture of a handsome brother. "He kinda looks like Jamal, huh?"

"Kinda," I said, and turned on the TV. "So, what's up with you and Jamal anyway?"

Emako fixed her eyes on me and hesitated, as if there were a right or wrong answer.

"I know you are not tryin' to get in my bizness, Monterey," she replied.

"I sure am," I said.

"That's only becuz you don't have no bizness of your own to be in." Emako laughed.

"You ain't funny. That's okay, Emako, go ahead and laugh, but it's Saturday night and here you are, sittin' up in here with me, getting ready to eat take-out pizza. So, like I said, what's up with you and Jamal?"

"Ain't nuthin' ro-man-tic. Besides, he has this girlfriend who goes to private school and lives in the hills and, according to Savannah, him and . . . Gina—that's her name—are wrapped up too tight. At least that's what Savannah tells me. She says she doesn't want my feelin's hurt."

"Why is Savannah all up in your life?"

"She said she was just tryin' to be nice."

"Savannah ain't nice. Even I know that," I replied.

"I know, but I kinda feel sorry for her," Emako said.

"Why?"

"Savannah don't seem very happy. You know . . . like, she never smiles or laughs."

"If I looked like her, I wouldn't be smilin' either. . . . Savannah is too ugly," I said, and changed the channel to BET, *Rap City*. Busta Rhymes was out of control. I got up to dance.

"Sit down, Monterey. You dance like a white girl."

"Hey!" I said. "Why you wanna diss me like that?"

"I'm just clownin' with you," Emako said.

I sat back down and turned the channel to MTV. "What you doin' tomorrow?" I asked.

"Drivin' up to Wayside to see my brother Dante. It's visitin' day. Once a month we go up there, sit around for a few hours, talkin' and laughin'. Don't misunderstand me. It ain't like some picnic in the park, but Mama misses him." Emako looked down. "When he first got sent there, I used to tell everyone that he went to Kansas to stay with my auntie, but everybody knew that I was lyin'. They knew where he really was. Besides, we don't even know nobody in Kansas. So I just started telling the truth. 'He's at Way-side.' I figured that if anyone had a problem with that, then I had a problem with them."

"What'd he do?" I asked.

"Gangbangin', ballin', got busted for dealin' dope and carryin' a concealed weapon and got two years. I figure he's better off there. If he was still home with my mama, he'd be in the ground. Mama said he's gonna get rehabilitated. She thinks he's gonna get out, go to some trade school, learn to be a plumber or something, and his past is gonna stop following him around, but I know it won't. Boys round our block won't let it. He's in too deep, so I know that he's just gonna get out and get shot or sent up again. Dante . . . he's got bad karma."

We stopped talking and watched television for a while.

My daddy knocked. "Pizza's here."

We sat down on the floor and opened the pizza box.

"I got a job at Burger King. I start next week." Emako smiled as she picked up a can of Mountain Dew.

"For real?" I asked.

"Yeah, for real . . . the BK that's right around the corner from my house. I put in a application at Popeye's Chicken too, but they wouldn't hire me because I didn't have no experience. Can you believe that? I spoze it's easier to learn to fry hamburgers than chicken. Anyway, it'll feel good to start putting a little change in my mama's pocket. She's been strugglin' since my daddy left."

"Where is he?"

"Gone," Emako replied.

"Gone where?"

"Just gone, Monterey. Been gone so long, my mama calls him Been Gone Bobby Blue. I think he's dead, but my mama said no. She said he's just another invisible man who knows how to get lost and stay lost unless he smells money. Then you turn around and see him walking down the street toward the house, wearing a suit, smilin' like he just got back from a vacation in Hawaii. And then, when the money runs out, he's gone again."

I looked down at my pizza. I didn't know what to say.

"Why you gotta look so sad? It ain't the end of my world. Besides, you wait and see. When I'm famous and livin' large, he'll show up with his hand out, ready to be my daddy, and you know what?"

"What?"

"I'm gonna tell him to get out my face."

Emako took a bite of her pizza and changed the subject. "So, what's going on with you and Eddie Ortiz? I always see you lookin' at him. I could ask Jamal to hook you up."

"You must be kiddin'. Eddie's a senior."

"But he's only sixteen and you need to stop bein' so shy around him."

"I get nervous," I said.

"Next time he tries to talk to you, just act normal. A'ight?"

"A'ight."

"He's tryin' to get early admission to college, at least that's what Jamal told me," Emako said.

"Someone told me he's real smart," I added.

"I'm serious. I could ask Jamal to hook you two up and then we could go somewhere, the four of us."

"My parents won't let me. Not until I'm sixteen."

"How come?"

"I dunno. They treat me like I'm still a little kid. Like I don't have good sense. Like they're afraid something bad's gonna happen. This summer I want to get a job, but they're sending me to some SAT summer camp."

"I'm sad for you, girlfriend. Real sad," Emako said, "but they seem kinda nice . . . your mama and daddy."

"I never said they weren't nice, but I still can't wait to get away from 'em."

Jamal

I had been trying to get tight with Emako, calling her almost every night, but she was always talking about the friendship thing. All I kept thinking was that I didn't need any more friends, at least not friends who looked like her.

It was a Saturday night, a couple of weeks before Christmas. I had picked up Emako after she got off work and we were riding, just riding through L.A., and somehow we found ourselves in Beverly Hills.

"Beverly Hills sure knows how to do Christmas," Emako said as we drove.

"Wanna walk around? We could stroll down Rodeo Drive, scare the white people." I laughed like the devil.

She tugged at her Burger King uniform and gave me a look as if to say, Dressed like this?

"Ain't nuthin', just Beverly Hills," I said, and parked.

We got out of the car and walked along the crowded sidewalks toward Rodeo, two dark faces in a sea of white.

"I got a question," I said.

"What?"

"Why in the hood do they say *Ro*deo like the rodeo where they ride wild horses, and in Beverly Hills they say Ro-*day*-o like it's a different country or something? I mean, what's up with that?"

"You crazy, Jamal."

We stopped in front of a jewelry store where the diamonds glistened like ice under the lights, and I took her small hand and held it. I said to myself, I think I'm in love.

"You gonna buy me some ice, Jamal?" Emako asked.

"It could be like that one day. After I start producin' my music and all that." I gazed deep into her brown eyes. "C'mon, let's go inside," I said, pulling her toward the front door.

She let go of my hand. "I'm not goin' in there and have them lookin' at me like I don't b'long. Which I don't. Why you gotta mess with me?"

"I'm not messin' with you. I just wanted to give 'em something to talk about when they go home tonight and turn on *Jay Leno*."

The security guard had come to the door and he was hovering.

"See. That's how it is. Soon as they see a black face, se-

curity is all up on us. Like I'm Bonnie and you're Clyde."
Emako shook her head. "Let's go."

We went back to the car, but before we got in, I pulled
her to me and kissed her. I could taste her strawberry lip
gloss. Her mouth was sweet and warm, just like I'd imagined.

We got in my ride and took off. It started to rain and
the streets were black and wet.

"You know, there's this girl named Gina," I said.

"I heard all about Gina," she replied.

"Savannah?" I asked.

"Savannah," she responded. "She said that you just tryin'
to be a player."

"I'm not tryin' to be a player, I'm just tryin' to be real
with you."

"And what about Gina? You gonna rush home and call
her on the phone and tell her all about me?"

I was silent, caught in my own game.

"Jamal? It's just a kiss, nuthin' but a kiss. I mean, if you
gotta get into true confessions, then okay, but I'm not about
that. What you think, one kiss makes me wanna have your
baby? It don't."

"Oh, it's like that?"

"Yeah, it's like that," Emako said, but I could tell she
wasn't mad.

The windshield wipers scraped the windows back and

forth like a metronome, and I remembered the born-again Christian piano teacher and the smell of soul food that always filled her house, and my mouth began to water.

"You hungry?" I asked.

"No. I'm tired. Just take me home."

"I wrote you some songs. Music and lyrics," I said.

"You wrote me some songs?"

"Yeah, for your first CD. We could go to my house. I got a keyboard, some recording stuff."

"And let me guess. Your mama 'n' daddy ain't home."

"Outta town."

"Yeah, you're real slick, Jamal. Take me home."

"Can't blame a brother for tryin'. But I did write the songs. I'm in love with music."

"You're in love with music?"

"Yeah, everything from Miles Davis to Jay-Z." I paused. "I love music almost as much as I love you."

"You think you're smooth, huh?"

"Yeah."

"Well, you ain't."

Savannah

The night of the Christmas concert we were all wearing white choir robes because Mr. Santos said he wanted us to look like angels. What a geek.

The auditorium was almost full and I searched the faces, looking for my mother and stepfather. I couldn't find them. They'd be late, as usual, so my mother could make her grand entrance, looking like a Patti LaBelle clone, my stepfather walking behind her with his shaved peanut head.

Mr. Santos approached the center of the stage and welcomed everyone. "It's my favorite time of the year," he said. He picked up his tuning forks and the lights went down.

Emako stepped forward and began to sing "Joy to the World."

She sounded better than Whitney. Even I had to admit it.

I pictured her on the MTV Music Awards, performing with three thick brown backup singers, another ghetto girl making it big, thanking God and her mama.

When she finished, the audience gave her a standing ovation. I took a deep breath and swallowed.

The auditorium door opened and in the darkness I could see my mother and stepfather. She had missed her grand entrance and I felt like laughing. They hurried down the center aisle and found seats. I was glad they had missed Emako's solo. Now I wouldn't have to hear it for the next month. "That girl sure can sing."

Emako took her place in the chorus and Mr. Santos hit the tuning fork. We began to sing "On the First Day of Christmas." Applause.

Then a spiritual, "O Happy Day." The crowd clapped again and I thought, I could get used to this.

Many more songs. More applause.

A solo from Eddie Ortiz, star tenor, "Danny Boy." Mr. Santos had tears in his eyes.

We ended with "We Wish You a Merry Christmas." The audience was on their feet.

We were that good.

My mother waved at me from her seat. I felt so good that I actually smiled at her.

Then it was over, and after we took our bows, Mr. Santos said, "See you next year, thank you for coming. Happy holidays. Drive safely."

As the audience began to rush out, a woman rushed up to Emako and held her tight. I figured it was her mother. They hugged for a long time, like they loved each other or something, and these two little kids were standing around them too. They had to be Emako's brother and sister. They looked alike. Pretty.

I scanned the faces for my mother, but I couldn't find her, and when I looked back toward Emako, Jamal was beside her, holding her hand like she belonged to him, and this short white dude was hovering around them. I heard someone say that he was from Aurora Records. He handed Emako's mother a card and introduced himself. Then he took Emako's other hand and shook it. Emako's face was all lit up and I thought, It's going to be just that easy for her. Easy like $1 + 1 = 2$.

My stepfather took me by the arm. "Your mother is already in the car." I followed him to the door, turning around for a last look at the small crowd that had gathered around Emako.

When we got outside, I got out my cell phone and punched in Gina's number.

The phone rang and Gina picked up. "Hello?"

"Where you at?"

"At that black-tie thing. Daddy made me."

"You are not gonna believe this. I just left our Christmas concert and there's this little dude here from Aurora Records, all up in Emako's face like she's about to walk down the road of fame and fortune."

"And . . . ?"

"Jamal's holdin' her hand like he's about to go with her."

Gina paused. "I can't talk right now."

"Whatever . . . but I don't think you are catchin' the seriousness of all this."

"Thank you, Savannah."

"Thank you? That's all you gotta say?"

"I'll call you later."

I put my cell phone in my purse and got in the car.

I began to wonder why I was all up in someone else's relationship. I mean, if Gina didn't care, then why should I?

"It was a wonderful concert, dear," my mother said to me later, from the front seat.

"Yeah . . . just wonderful," I replied.

■ ■ ■

The very next night, Gina and Jamal had what you would call a major confrontation and she called me, crying.

"What's wrong?" I asked.

"We broke up." She sounded too pitiful.

"Right b'fore Christmas. That figures." Now she wouldn't even get a present, I thought. "What happened?"

"He said he just wasn't feelin' it . . . you know, me and him."

"Yeah, but he's feelin' Emako, right?"

"He said it didn't have anything to do with her."

"And you wanna believe that? Even you're not that stupid."

"Why you wanna say that?"

"Becuz all he ever did was play you from the beginning."

Gina was silent for a moment. "I thought you were my friend, Savannah."

"I am your friend, but Jamal ain't all that."

"But I still love him."

"Why?"

"Cuz he's fine," she replied, and started crying again.

I took a deep breath and sighed. I know she doesn't think I want to listen to this madness all night. "I'm getting sleepy, Gina. I'll call you tomorrow . . . okay?"

"Fine. Bye," she said. I could tell she was pissed.

Eddie

Two days before Christmas I went to find a present for my baby sister, Hortensia. It was crowded and people bumped into one another like it was expected.

"Eddie!" someone yelled behind me.

I turned around and saw Monterey and Emako.

"What up, Monterey? Hey, Emako," I said.

"Hey, Eddie," they responded at the same time, smiling.

"It's crowded, huh?" I said.

"It's two days before Christmas, what you expect?" Emako said. "You here to buy us some presents, Eddie?"

I looked at Emako with a question in my eyes.

Monterey answered. "She's just clownin' with you, Eddie. You know she's crazy."

She spoke to me, I thought. Finally!

"I forgot," I said, laughing.

Emako stared at my Arizona State sweatshirt. "You goin' to Arizona State?" she asked.

"I dunno yet. I applied to ten schools."

"Which ones?" Monterey asked as we made our way slowly through the crowd.

"All outta state. I gotta get away from here before . . ."

"Before what?" Monterey asked.

"Before I wind up just another *cholo* like my brother."

"I understand," Emako said.

"What's wrong with L.A.?" Monterey asked us.

"Not much if you live where you live," Emako replied.

"Oh . . . it's like that," Monterey said. "I ain't rich."

"But you ain't poor and you don't havta worry about going outside your house after dark," Emako said.

"Or gettin' nervous whenever a car slows down," I added.

"Be quiet, Eddie. You don't even know where I live." Monterey sounded like she was getting mad.

Emako turned to Monterey. "One day when you start to grow up, you might see how it really is, but right now you're blinded by your perfect little world."

"My perfect little world?"

"That's what I said," Emako replied, and walked on ahead, leaving me behind with Monterey. She stopped in front of a store called Forever 21 and peered in the window.

"Why you gotta talk to me like that!" Monterey raised her voice.

"Don't get all mad," Emako said, and entered the store.

Monterey looked pissed, so I tried to change the subject. "I gotta find a present for my baby sister, but I don't know what to get her."

"I didn't know you had a little sister. How old is she?" Monterey asked.

"She's nine."

"Get her a gift certificate. That's what I got Emako, but don't tell her," Monterey said.

"I won't."

"One day she's gonna be famous," Monterey said.

"Who?" I asked.

"Emako. Somebody called her mother from Aurora Records," Monterey whispered like it was a secret. "They were at the Christmas concert."

"Cool," I replied.

"But her mama told 'em that Emako was gonna havta finish high school b'fore she signs any contract. Don't say nuthin' becuz I promised not to tell anyone."

"I promise." I looked at Monterey. Her eyes and hair were almost black. Her skin was the color of caramel. Her lips were shiny pink. Suddenly, I decided to do it. "I could call you if I had your phone number," I said.

She looked surprised. "Huh?"

"I said, I could call you if I had your phone number."

"Okay," she said, and smiled at me really big, showing her braces. She took a pen and some paper out of her purse, wrote it down with a smiley face, and handed it to me.

I put it in my wallet so I wouldn't lose it.

I felt really good.

I looked over the railing down to the first floor, where a big white man wearing a Santa suit was sitting on a golden throne like a king. A line of children waited their turn to whisper wishes in his ear.

"Remember when you used to believe in Santa?" I asked.

"What?" Monterey replied.

"I said, remember—?"

"I heard what you said. You mean, Santa ain't real?" Monterey was trying hard to look serious, but her lips parted and she grinned again.

Emako came back toward us.

"Emako? Did you know there ain't no such thing as Santa Claus?"

"I thought you were mad."

"Well, I should be, but I ain't," Monterey said.

"I'm sorry." Emako smiled. "You know I'm just playin' with you."

"I know," Monterey said as the three of us bumped our way through the swarm of shoppers.

"I still don't know what to get her," I said. "Maybe I'll just give her a Christmas card and stick twenty dollars in it."

"For who?" Emako asked.

"His little sister. She's nine." Monterey answered.

"Get her a Barbie doll. That's what I got for my baby sister. They pro'bly still have some good ones at that toy store on the lower level," Emako said as a man pushed up against her and almost made her trip.

"That's a good idea," I said.

A little boy stepped on Emako's foot. "Ouch! There are too many people up in here. Let's go."

Monterey agreed. "Okay."

"I gotta get the Barbie doll," I said.

"Later, Eddie. Merry Christmas," Emako said.

"Yeah, Eddie, *Feliz Navidad*," Monterey added.

"Feliz Navidad," I repeated as they made their way toward the exit doors. I watched them until they vanished, swallowed by the crowd.

A woman ran into me with a stroller without apologizing, but I didn't get upset, because it was Christmas and her baby was crying.

I opened my wallet and stared at Monterey's phone number.

Monterey

My phone was ringing. I rubbed my eyes and looked at the clock. It was 6:30 in the morning, Saturday, January 11, my birthday. "Hello?"

"You asleep?" Emako asked.

"What you think? It's Saturday."

"Happy birthday," she said, and laughed.

I groaned. "Later, Emako. You ain't funny."

"But I got a present for you. I'll be over there after work. You gonna be home?"

"Yeah, my mama is making me a birthday cake with sixteen candles and my nana's comin' over and some of my little cousins and my auntie and uncle."

"Princess Monterey."

"Good-bye, Emako."

"Later."

I hung up the phone and stared at the ceiling. I was sixteen, but I didn't feel any different. I turned over, closed my eyes, and went back to sleep.

■ ■ ■

When the phone rang again at 8:30, I thought it was Emako. "I'm still tryin' to sleep, Emako."

"Hey, Monterey. It's Eddie."

I sat up in bed. It was the third time he'd called since I'd seen him in the mall. "Hey, Eddie. I thought you were Emako."

"It's kind of early. I could call you back later."

"No. It's okay."

"Happy birthday," he said.

"Who told you it was my birthday? Emako, huh?"

"Yeah. . . . Are you, like, havin' a party or anything?" he asked.

"Just my mama and daddy and some cousins and stuff . . . nuthin' special. I could ask if you could come over if you want to."

"I can't. I have to work today in my father's market . . . but maybe next week I could meet you at the mall."

"They might be cool with that."

"I'll see you at school on Monday."

"Okay," I replied.

"Later, Monterey. Happy birthday."

"Later, Eddie," I said, and hung up the phone. I was too happy. I put my head back on my pillow and tried to close my eyes. Sixteen was already feeling pretty good.

■ ■ ■

Most of the day was boring. All my little cousins wanted to do was play video games on my computer. My nana forgot to put batteries in her hearing aids, so everyone was talking too loud. I was glad they went home early.

It was 5:30 in the afternoon when Emako rang the doorbell and handed me a small box.

"Happy birthday."

"You didn't have to get me anything," I said as she walked through the door.

"But I did," she replied.

My daddy looked up from the TV. "Hi, Emako."

"Hey, Mr. Hamilton," she said.

My mama peeked her head out of the kitchen. "Hi, Emako."

"Hey, Miz Hamilton."

"I keep telling you, call me DeeDee. Everybody does," my mother said.

"DeeDee," Emako repeated.

We went into my room and closed the door.

"I forgot a card," she apologized.

"Don't matter." I tore off the wrapping paper and opened the box. It was the silver bracelet I had wanted the time we had gone to Melrose. "I can't believe this! You re-membered!"

"I remembered."

I put on the bracelet. "You my bestest girl." I looked at the bracelet on my arm. "I cannot believe you did this! This is too sweet! You want some birthday cake?"

"Maybe later."

"You could have gumbo if you want, but my daddy ate most of the shrimp."

"Not right now." She got up and went over to my CD rack. "Could I borrow your Jay-Z CD?"

"It's there. Daddy said he's gonna get me a CD burner. Then I'll be able to make my own CDs."

She put the CD in and began to sing along. Then she stopped singing and sat down. She looked sad.

"What's wrong?" I asked.

"Some knucklehead came into my line at work today, lookin' for my brother. You remember the little gangsta you said was fine? Who was drivin' that Regal outside my house when you first came over?"

"Who was in CYA?"

"Yeah, him."

"And . . . ?"

"And I told him that he knew where Dante was and he needed to get out my face unless he wanted to order some-thin' to eat."

"And . . . ?"

"So he looks in my eyes real hard like he's tryin' to scare the black off me and orders a Whopper with cheese and a large drink, pays for it, makin' sure that I see all the ice on his fingers, and the Rolex on his wrist, you know, like bling-bling, goes outside, and gets in his ride."

"Were you scared?"

"I ain't scared of nuthin'. Just sometimes I wish Dante would disappear and never come back."

"You love him?" I asked.

"He's my brother. I just hope Marcel don't get caught up in any mess, cuz he's a cool little dude."

"He is," I said.

"He ain't nuthin' like Dante. I think Dante was just born mean. But I love Marcel with his goofy little self. Always clownin'." Emako had a little smile on her face.

I couldn't wait any longer. "Eddie called me," I blurted.

"Again?"

"Yeah, this morning, to say happy birthday, and then he said maybe we could meet at the mall on Saturday."

"Eddie's kinda cool," Emako said.

"He is," I replied.

Eddie

One day at the beginning of January, I went to the school office to have my transcripts sent to the U of New Mexico, and there she was. Emako.

"So what's up, superstar?" I said.

"Superstar?" she asked.

"You know, what's up with Aurora Records?" I asked, forgetting my vow of secrecy. "Oops. I promised Monterey I wouldn't say anything."

"It's okay. Everybody knows anyway. Can you believe it? But my mama says I can't even go near a recording studio till I graduate."

"Maybe she'll change her mind."

"No, she won't, becuz she said someone is gonna graduate from high school and that someone is gonna be me. Plus, I wanna be a good example for my little brother and sister. It's a responsibility thing, you know?"

"Ain't nuthin', just two more years," I said.

"Can I help you?" the office lady said from behind the counter.

"I need to have my transcripts sent," I replied.

"Again? And where to this time, Mr. Ortiz?"

"New Mexico. They want to see my mid-semester progress reports."

"Didn't you apply for early admission to Arizona State?" she asked.

"Yeah, I'll know by January fifteenth, but just in case."

"It's your life, Mr. Ortiz. Here's the form. And you, miss?" she said to Emako.

"I was absent yesterday, but I forgot to come to the office and get my slip, and Miz Warren said I could come and get it after school becuz I was almost late this morning and we had a history quiz and she didn't want me to miss the quiz so—"

"Enough . . . too much information. Reason for absence?"

"I was sick."

She filled the out the absence slip and signed it. "Bring this to homeroom tomorrow."

"Thank you," Emako said, and turned to leave. "Later, Eddie."

"I'll bring this back tomorrow," I said, holding up the transcript form.

"Like I said, it's your life, Mr. Ortiz. Just don't come in here blaming me like you did last week because your grades didn't get there in time and now your life is ruined forever because you have to go to the junior college down the street."

Her words made me think again. "Okay, I'll do it now," I said, watching Emako walk out the door into the hallway.

The office lady sat back at her desk. "Like I said, Mr. Ortiz, it's your life."

I scribbled in my info as fast as I could and she took it from my hand like she had won a victory.

When I got outside, Emako was standing there with Jamal. "It's your life, Mr. Ortiz," she mimicked.

Jamal nodded. "Hey, Eddie."

"Hey, Jamal," I replied.

"I hear you gonna hook up with sweet Monterey this weekend," Jamal said.

"She's not sure yet."

"Her moms and pops?" Jamal asked.

"Yeah." I felt a little embarrassed. "I gotta go before I miss my bus."

"Bye, Eddie," Emako said.

"Later," I said, and left them by the lockers.

I stopped at the 7-Eleven and bought a Mountain Dew and some pork rinds for my ride home, then headed back to the bus stop. I was early, so I sat on the bench and started to eat.

I heard them first. The music was loud enough to wake up a corpse.

They were driving a Chevy with tinted windows.

They slowed down and I felt the fear. I whispered a prayer, asking God to protect me. I didn't want a bullet in my spine or head. I wanted to see my future. I was innocent. Innocence had to count for something.

The Chevy came to a stop in front of me.

The window rolled down and I took a deep breath.

This is a mistake. I'm not Tomas.

The passenger flashed a gang sign and I shrugged my shoulders.

He looked at me and laughed as he rolled up the window.

The Chevy roared away and I breathed.

It felt like I sat there forever. Finally, I could see my bus in the distance coming toward me. I climbed aboard and sat down next to a little old lady, who nodded at me. She reminded me of my mother and I felt safe.

I got off the bus at the stop two blocks from my house. I hurried home, staring straight ahead.

I went around to the side of the house and came in through the open back door and locked it. My sister was in her room, watching TV. I headed for the kitchen, past the little altar with the statue of Jesus and the candle that my mother kept lit twenty-four hours a day, seven days a week. Behind them sat a picture of my brother, Tomas, when he was twelve years old.

My mother was in the kitchen cooking. *"Mijo,"* she sighed.

"You should keep the doors locked, even in the daytime! Something could happen!" I was almost yelling.

"Twenty-five years, nothing has happened. You worry too much, *Mijo*." She put the lid on the pot and wiped her hands on her apron.

I wanted her to put her arms around me the way she used to when I was a little boy.

"Sit down," she said. "I made some soup."

I sat down.

But the Chevy was still on my mind.

Savannah

Even if Gina didn't blame Emako, I did, and so I was on her back when school started up again.

Emako was in my public speaking class, and every time she got up to talk, I disrespected her from the back of the room, calling her the ghetto superstar and Emako the ho.

I guess Emako got tired of it, because one day after class she followed me out into the hall.

"Savannah!" she called.

There was something about the way she said my name, and I thought twice before I turned around. I decided to play innocent and smiled at her. "Hey, Emako."

"Why you gotta be like that?"

"Like what?" I replied.

"Like every time I get up to talk, you gotta make fun of me like you still back in the seventh grade."

"I'm just playin' with you. Don't be so sensitive."

She got all up in my face and said softly, "I'm not bein' sensitive. If you don't like me, I'm cool with that. I mean, it's not gonna keep me from sleepin' at night, you hear what I'm sayin'?"

"I got ears."

The bell rang and she walked away.

■ ■ ■

After school, I got a ride home with this girl named Jo'nelle who sat behind me in history class. We weren't really friends, but she lived around the corner from me and her mother sometimes gave me a ride home when my mother and stepfather were out of town. I sat in the backseat while her mother rattled on nonstop.

Let me out of here, I thought.

They dropped me off at the corner and I walked the rest of the way to my house. When I opened the door, Lillie started her dance around my feet, barking. She looked like an overgrown rat with long hair. I locked her in the service porch. If she's lucky, I thought, I might feed her . . . later.

My mother and stepfather were in Thailand and I was home alone, again. I called Pizza Hut and ordered a large pepperoni pizza. While I waited, I got a Coors out of the refrigerator and took a swallow.

I looked in the small mirror that hung over the sink and toasted myself. Today was my sixteenth birthday.

By the time the pizza came, I had finished two cans of beer and I was high. I stumbled to the door and paid for the pizza.

"Today's my birthday," I told the delivery guy. "Keep the change."

"Hey, thanks," he said, "and happy birthday."

I closed the door, went back into the kitchen, and let Lillie out of the service porch. I opened another can of beer and poured some in her empty water bowl. She lapped it up and I started to laugh. I sat down, took out a slice for Lillie and a slice for me. She jumped in my lap and licked my face.

"Happy birthday, Savannah," I said as I hugged the little dog.

The phone rang and I jumped. I smiled as I picked up the phone, thinking it was my mother. "Hello?"

It was Gina. I wanted to cry. "Hi, Gina."

"Happy birthday, girl," she said.

"Yeah," I replied.

"You don't sound too happy. What's up with you? It's your birthday. Did you get a car?"

"No. My mother and the man are in Thailand."

"Oh. Maybe they'll get it for you when they come back," she said.

I knew she was trying to make me feel good. "Yeah, maybe," I replied.

"You want me to come over?"

"No, I'm cool." I didn't need anyone feeling sorry for me.

There was a long pause. "How's Jamal?"

"Is that why you really called, to ask about Jamal?"

"I called to say happy birthday. Why you gotta be nasty?"

I took another gulp of beer. "Sorry. Jamal is fine."

"Oh . . . ," she said, and hesitated. "Is he gettin' tight with Emako?"

"Yes."

"You think I should call him?"

"Do whatever you want, but don't come cryin' to me again if he hurts your feelings, okay?"

There was silence.

"I won't," she replied. "Bye."

"Later."

Jamal

I was in my room, trying to study for a math test. I had my headphones on and I was listening to the music, staying out of trouble, staying off the streets. Every time you turned around, someone was getting shot in L.A., and I didn't want my name added to the growing list. There were times when it made me jumpy. Not scared—just jumpy.

It was like you could just be out in your ride with the music bumpin', thinking you had a bright future as a music producer or something, and then a car rolls by slowly and Bang! Bang! Bang! The lights go out and you ain't going nowhere except to the emergency room in the back of an ambulance or to the morgue in a zipped-up black body bag. People left standing around talking to the media who claim you were "gang related" when the only thing you were related to were your moms and pops, who now only have your picture to look at for the rest of their lives. It made a young brother tense.

As for me, my life was smooth, and I wanted it to stay that way.

It was 10:15. I had promised to call Emako. I closed the book, took off my headset, and picked up the phone. It rang four times before her little brother answered.

"Hello?" Marcel said.

"Is Emako home?" I asked.

"Yeah, she's home," he answered.

"Can I holler at her?"

"Just a minute," he said, and yelled, "Emako!"

I sat and waited.

"Gimme the phone," I heard her say. "And get your little butt in the bed. . . ." A pause. "Hello?"

"Hey, Emako," I said.

"Hey."

"What you doin'?"

"Nuthin'," she replied.

"You wanna do somethin' on Saturday?" I asked.

"Like what?"

"Whatever."

There was a very long pause. "Jamal?"

"Yeah?"

"Did you really break it off with Gina?"

"Would I lie to you? You wanna do somethin' on Saturday or not?" I asked.

"Or what . . . you gonna call Gina and ask her?"

"Why you gotta be like that? I told you I'm finished with all that."

"I got a question for you."

"Okay."

"When's that last time you talked to Gina?"

"Last night."

"Why you tryin' to be a player?"

"I'm not tryin' to be a player no more. I'm just tryin' to keep it real. Besides, she called me."

"G'night, Jamal."

"So, I'll see you Saturday?"

"Maybe. . . . G'night."

"G'night." I hung up the phone, looked one last time at the math book on the floor, and turned off the light. Emako wasn't the type to sit around and be played, I thought. She just might be the one to make me change my ways. I closed my eyes and fell asleep.

Monterey

"I'm gonna take these braids out this weekend. I'm tired of 'em. I've had 'em so long, I forgot what I look like without 'em. I think I'll get it cut real short and dye it platinum blond like Eve," Emako said one day after chorus.

I tried to picture it. "That might look dope."

"Dope? Why don't you just talk like the square that you are? You worse than that girl on BET slingin' ghetto slang."

"Why you always gotta criticize me? Like you're tryin' to make me feel bad. I'm gettin' tired of it."

"Don't get all mad," Emako said.

"That's what you always say. I'm gettin' tired of that too."

"Okay. I'm sorry. Talk any way you wanna talk. Ain't nuthin'."

"Besides, I gotta talk like that. You never know. One day it could be me. *106 & Park*. Live from New York," I said.

"I said sorry." She looked at me like she was sincere. "You know it could be like that," she added.

"For real, huh?"

"For real," she replied.

Her bus came and I watched her hurry away. She turned around and waved at me and I felt better.

My daddy pulled up a few minutes later.

"Your mother has her night class tonight, so I was going to cook," he said as I crawled in.

"Please don't."

"Why?"

"Becuz you can't cook."

"I can't cook?"

"Not really."

"Well then, maybe you could cook, Monterey."

"I can't cook either. Can't we just stop and get KFC?"

"Okay, but don't tell your mother. I promised her that I would make you eat healthy food."

"I won't tell her."

"How was school?" he asked.

"It was a'ight."

He corrected me. "You mean all right."

"That's what I said, a'ight."

He looked at me and shook his head.

As soon as we got home, I loaded up a paper plate with fried chicken, mashed potatoes and gravy, and two biscuits. I poured some cold Pepsi into a paper cup.

"We could sit down and eat like a family," my daddy said.

"That's okay, maybe tomorrow," I replied, and went into my room. I locked my door, turned on *TRL*, and got busy with the food.

That's how my days were, nothing special, no drama. Maybe Emako was right about my perfect life.

I took a bite of chicken.

The phone rang and I picked it up. "Hello?"

It was Emako. "Monterey?"

"Yeah?" Now my food's going to get cold, I thought.

"You are not going to believe who just called me."

I picked up the remote and pushed mute. "Who?"

"Gina."

"Jamal's Gina?"

"Jamal's ex-Gina."

"No she did not! Who gave her your number?"

"I give you one guess."

"Savannah?"

"Savannah."

I put down my food. "And?"

"She told me I needed back up off Jamal."

"What?"

"And I told her that she should be talkin' to Jamal, not me."

"And what'd she say then?"

"Somethin' about me bein' a ho, and that was when I told her that the conversation was over . . . click, and I hung up the phone."

"I cannot believe her."

"Who you tellin'? Like it's my fault. Plus, ain't nuthin' even happened between Jamal and me. At least nuthin' like what she thinks. The most we ever did was kiss."

"So what you gonna do?"

"I'm 'bout to call Jamal."

"Then call me back, okay? And I want the whole story."

"Later."

I hung up the phone and picked up my food again. It was still warm.

Twenty minutes later, my phone rang.

"Hey," Emako said.

"And . . . ?"

"Jamal said he was gonna talk to Gina and tell her not to call me

al sweet . . . tryin' to be smooth."

"You're getting into him, huh?" I asked.

"He's a'ight."

"I thought you didn't have time for no mess."

"I don't. But he's kinda fine."

I agreed, "He is."

"He asked me to go to Disneyland this weekend."

"You goin'?"

"I dunno, maybe. . . ." She paused. "I gotta go. I promised to help Marcel with his multiplication b'fore he gets too sleepy. See ya t'morrow."

"Later," I replied.

Jamal

She had never been to Disneyland. Never. I couldn't believe it. At first she had said she wouldn't go because of all this drama with Gina. But she finally said okay.

We walked through the gates of the Magic Kingdom and her eyes were all wide like she was a little girl.

I felt like I was opening up the world for her.

I felt like a man.

I took her hand and held it like she was mine.

Emako had taken the braids out of her hair, cut it real short, and dyed it blond. She looked good.

"The first thing I gotta do is buy Marcel and Latrice those Mickey Mouse hats with their names embroidered on 'em. I promised," she said.

"Wait till we get ready to leave, cuz that way you won't have to carry 'em around with you all day. That's one of the big mistakes people make when they come to Disneyland, and then when they go on Space Mountain and all the good rides, they gotta worry 'bout holdin' on to a bag, worryin' 'bout stuff fallin' out," I said as we walked toward Fantasyland.

"Okay, but don't let me forget."

"I promise," I said, taking her hand.

We stayed from ten o'clock in the morning until eleven o'clock at night. The new Disney adventure, the old Disney adventure, the whole Disney adventure. I was glad when she finally got tired.

The freeway wasn't crowded and the ride put her to sleep. She looked like a sleeping doll. I stopped the car in front of her house and she woke up, startled. I pulled her to me and kissed her lips. She kissed me back, but I started getting hot and my hands started traveling and she froze.

"Stoppit, Jamal," she said softly, but I knew she meant it. She opened the car door and got out.

"You mad?" I asked, getting out to walk her to the door.

"I ain't mad."

The lights were all out in her house. She put her key in the lock of the rusting security door and turned around.

"Thank you, Jamal . . . for takin' me to Disneyland. It was fun."

"Yeah, it was."

I got back in the car and locked the doors. I was in South L.A. and it was after midnight.

The porch light was on when I got home. I tiptoed in. The house was quiet like the night before Christmas.

I stripped down to my boxers and got between the sheets. I thought about Emako. I had almost stopped noticing the other honeys and I called her every night. Oh, hell, no. I'm in way too deep. I shook my head and closed my eyes. Sleep didn't take its time finding me.

Eddie

Finally! I got my early acceptance from Arizona State. Now I was smiling all the time. I couldn't wait to leave Los Angeles behind me. Sometimes it felt like this city was about to swallow me up whole like a hungry python.

Emako sat down beside me in the cafeteria.

"I got accepted at Arizona State," I announced.

"Congratulations, Eddie! Arizona State, cool."

"Yeah," I said. "My parents are all proud. My dad put up a big sign in his market. I never heard the word *mijo* so much in my life before."

"*Mijo?*"

"My son," I translated.

"So you gonna come back and visit us?" she asked.

"Maybe." She had a strange look in her eyes. "What's up?" I asked.

"Someone put a knife in my brother Dante, but he ain't dead."

"Where is he?"

"Wayside."

"My brother, Tomas, was there three years ago. Now he's at Chino. He's been shot and stabbed so many times that we stopped calling him the cat with nine lives and started calling him the cat with twenty-nine lives. He just keeps on living."

"Karma," she said.

"Yeah," I replied. "All he does is worry my mother. She hardly sleeps. I find her in the morning, curled up on the sofa, the TV on, rosary in her hands, tears in her eyes. Last time I saw him he had tracks on both arms . . . heroin, and I said, 'Dude, you gonna get HIV.' He looked like someone had stolen his soul. That was when I decided to try and forget him, but I can't."

"My mama keeps telling me that God's gonna answer her prayers, but her hair is turnin' white from worryin'," Emako said. "Now he might get an early release. You know, time served. That's all we need, Dante back up in the house, bringin' us down."

I reached for Emako's hand. She took my hand and held it. Tears began to well up in her eyes, but she held them back and let go of my hand.

"Ain't nuthin'," she said.

"Yeah," I replied. She was strong like me. "It's gonna be good, for me and you. In two years you'll have your recording contract and be outta here too."

"A lot can happen in two years, Eddie."

Monterey sat down beside me. "What's up, y'all?"

"Nuthin', 'cept Mr. Eddie got accepted to Arizona State," Emako replied.

"I know," Monterey said, and looked up at me.

"I called her yesterday as soon as I got the letter," I added.

"Why do you look so sad?" Monterey asked.

"Emako's brother got stabbed," I told Monterey.

"I know," Monterey said. "But he's gonna be okay."

"Every time I turn around, it's more DD," Emako said.

"DD?" I asked.

"Dante's Drama," she replied. We all laughed.

"One more summer and I'm outta here. L.A. will be history. Nuthin' about this city that I'm gonna miss," I said.

Monterey and Emako looked at each other.

"Except you guys," I added.

Monterey moved closer to me. "I was about to say."

"You two make a good couple," Emako said.

"We do?" I asked.

"We do," Monterey answered.

Savannah

When I saw Jamal's face on Monday and found out about the trip to Disneyland, I figured he was doing Emako. I mean, why else would he be so nice to her? So, I put the word out. Besides, if it hadn't been for Emako, Jamal and Gina would still be cool and I wouldn't have to listen to all of her pitiful nonsense almost every night.

Two days later, I was waiting for my mother after school and Jamal walks up to me like he's my best friend or something. I knew I was in trouble.

"Hey, Savannah," he said.

I wondered if I should run, but I remembered my first rule: When you find yourself in a bad situation, there is only one thing to do, lie.

"Hey, Jamal," I replied.

"How you been?"

"Everything's cool, waitin' on my mom. She's late."

He stared at me for a minute and then he spoke. "Did I ever tell you that you have a pretty mouth?"

It wasn't the kind of question that I expected. "No," I replied.

"Well, you do, and I was just wonderin'."

I thought to myself, I know he is not gonna get nasty with me. "Wonderin' what?"

"Wonderin' why you gotta use it to spread lies."

"Excuse me? I do not spread lies."

"Let me explain something to you, Savannah. Number one, I'm not doin' Emako, but that's really not your bizness, is it?"

"No," I said.

"Number two, next time you see Emako, I want you to tell her that you're sorry becuz she ain't about that, okay? Number three, stop callin' Gina with your nonsense."

"Why you think it's me? Like I'm the only one with a tongue," I said.

He shook his head and turned to walk away, still talking, "Y'all see a brother bein' nice to someone, and the first thing y'all wanna say is he's doin' her. And Savannah, one other thing."

"What?"

"Stay outta my face."

I looked around to see if anyone was watching, but there was no one. Two minutes later my mother drove up. I slithered into the front seat like the snake that I was.

"You can't speak when you get in the car?" she said.

"I said hi," I lied.

We drove in silence. This thing with Jamal and Emako, I thought, I'm never going to win, so I might as well give it up. If you ask me why I cause trouble, I would answer, I don't know. It used to be fun.

She dropped me off in front of the house and headed back to her travel agency. People were making their plans for the summer and it was busy.

I walked into the house and looked at my reflection in the mirror in the entryway. I was getting fat and I was too mean. No wonder no one loves me.

Monterey

The day Dante came home, my daddy dropped me off at Emako's house at about two o'clock in the afternoon. I knocked and Verna opened the door. She went out onto the porch in her robe and waved at my daddy while I snuck into the house.

Dante was asleep on the sofa. Emako had told me that they had given him an early release. He groaned and I saw him open one eye and then close it. His hair was corn-rowed, his skin dark brown. He pulled the covers over his head.

Emako yelled from her room, "I just got home from church! I gotta change my clothes!"

Dante groaned again and turned over.

I stood at the door and watched my daddy's car as it drove away.

Verna came back in the house. "I was making hot links and scrambled eggs. Have some?"

"No, thank you, Mrs. Blue. I already ate."

"What'd I tell you 'bout callin' me Mrs. Blue?"

"Verna."

"That's better."

Emako came into the living room. She was dressed in low-rider jeans and a white shirt. "C'mon," she said to me.

"Where y'all goin'?" Verna asked.

"Burger King. I gotta pick up my check. We'll be right back. C'mon, Monterey."

I followed her outside. The old man who lived next door was cutting his lawn with a push mower, and clumps of green grass lay on the sidewalk.

"You saw Dante," she said.

"Yeah, I saw him."

"His wound's infected, so my mama's been waitin' on him hand and foot like he's some kinda invalid, which he's not. I'll be glad when he gets well so he can get up outta my mama's house."

"Where's he gonna go?"

"I dunno, away . . . before he brings more trouble."

We walked to the corner and crossed the street.

"I got a tattoo." I rolled up my sleeve and showed her the vine of ivy that circled my upper arm.

"When?"

"Last Saturday. I took the bus to Venice, by myself."

"By yourself?" Emako paused. "Your mama's gonna kick your butt."

"It wears off in three weeks," I said.

"Henna?"

"Yeah."

"Your mama's still gonna kick your butt."

"Not like she needs to see me naked," I said.

"Monterey?"

"That's my name," I replied.

"I know you are not tryin' to get funky with me."

"I can and I did."

"So it's like that. One tattoo and a trip to Venice Beach and you grown?"

"I'm grown."

"A'ight then," she said, and smiled as we entered Burger King.

Emako headed toward the small office while I waited in front. I looked at the tattoo again and thought, I am grown. Almost.

She returned with her check, waving it like it was a hundred-dollar bill.

"C'mon." She motioned and we headed back out onto the streets. The sun was shining. The sky was blue.

We turned the corner toward her house. Dante was on the porch with three brothers.

"See what I mean?"

I did. "Yeah."

"But you can't tell my mama nuthin'. 'He's still my child,' is what she says. 'He's still my child,' over and over again."

We walked up the path to the front door.

"Baby sis," Dante said, and smiled. He was fine, but one of his front teeth was missing, looking like a black hole in his mouth.

The skin on the back of my neck stood up.

"Miz Emako . . . all grown up . . . ain't you fine," one of the brothers said, looking us both over from head to foot. "And who's your cute little friend?" All four of them laughed.

"Get out my way, J.T.," Emako snarled.

"Oh, it's like that?" J.T. snarled back.

"Yeah, it's like that," Emako replied.

Finally, Dante spoke up. "Leave the superstar and her little friend alone."

"Superstar!" they said in unison.

Emako pushed the door open and we went inside. "Mama, I thought he was supposed to be laying low. I mean, if he's well enough to walk outside and kick it with his gangstas, then he's well enough to get up outta here."

"He's still my child," was her mother's reply. "Y'all hungry?"

"No, we're not hungry. C'mon, Monterey."

We went into her room and she closed the door. "Can't

even have a normal life with him around. I gotta get outta here."

"You will."

"Yeah"—she took a deep breath—"I will." After a while she said, "Me and Jamal spozed to go to City Walk tonight. You wanna come? Maybe Eddie can come too."

"Yeah, but I gotta call my daddy," I replied.

She grinned at me. "Oh . . . but you grown."

She got up and I followed her into the living room. "Mama, where's the phone?"

"I dunno, ask Dante."

Emako went to the front door.

"Dante!"

"What?" Dante was standing on the sidewalk with J.T. The other two brothers were nowhere in sight.

"You got the phone?"

Dante held up the cordless black phone for her to see.

"Could I use it?"

"Come and get it, superstar."

Emako whispered something under her breath and stormed toward Dante and J.T. I trailed behind her.

Just then a car drove by. It was the same caramel-colored brother in the Regal that I'd seen before. The one who'd come into Emako's line at Burger King, looking for Dante. He stared at Dante. Dante nodded at him as he handed the phone to Emako.

The car rolled to the end of the block. Suddenly, the

brother in the Regal made a fast U-turn and drove back toward us. "Dante!" he yelled.

Dante looked up.

I froze when I saw the gun.

"Mama!" Emako screamed as the bullet hit her.

Dante and J.T. hit the ground and five more shots rang
out. When they ended, I was still frozen, watching the
Regal as it sped out of sight.

Dante and J.T. stood up, examining their bodies for
wounds. Emako's was on the sidewalk, lying in a small pool
of blood. Her eyes were wide open.

Verna raced out the door toward Emako, screaming.

She got down on her hands and knees and tried to pick
her up. She couldn't. "Call 911! Call 911!" she yelled, and
started to breathe air into Emako's mouth.

She reached up and grabbed me by the hand. "Push on
her chest."

I kneeled on the ground and pressed on Emako's chest.
Blood was all over my hands. "Wake up," I said softly.

Verna ran to a neighbor's house, still screaming, "Call
911!" She banged on the door until somebody opened it.

Dante and J.T. took off down the street. Marcel and
Latrice ran out of the house and stood over Emako's body.

"Wake up," I said again, but I knew she was dead.

The neighbors began to come out of their houses. I
heard sirens. The paramedics got there first. They formed

a shield around Emako, working fast. "It's too late. She's gone," one of them said.

The police got there next. Most of the people from the block disappeared into their houses. The yellow tape went up. The paramedics put a blanket over the body. Verna looked crazy. Latrice was crying.

Marcel yelled, "It's all Dante's fault!"

I went into the house and called Daddy. I kept staring at my bloody hands.

I watched the blood as I washed it off my hands down the drain. It looked like red wine.

Then, my mama and daddy were there. I talked to the police and Mama and Daddy put me in the car and took me home. Mama stood outside my bathroom while I took a shower. Daddy threw my bloody clothes away.

I felt like I was in a dream.

Jamal

Emako and I were supposed to go to City Walk. I called her house at 5:30, but there was no answer and I figured that she was out somewhere. The answering machine was off, so I couldn't leave a message.

I called back again at 6:30 and let it ring twenty times before I hung up.

At 7:00 I called a third time. It rang ten times and I was about to hang up when Marcel picked up the phone.

"Hello?" he said.

"Hey, little dude, let me talk to Emako."

"She ain't here."

"Tell her to call me when she gets home, okay?"

"She can't," he said.

"Why?" I asked.

"Cuz she got shot and now she's dead."

"Stop playin', Marcel."

"I'm not playin'. It's even on the TV. They came to shoot Dante, but he ain't dead or nuthin'. Then the ambulance came and tried to make her get better, but they couldn't."

"Wher's your moms?"

"She can. come to the phone cuz the doctor gave her some medicine and she's sleepin', but my auntie's here if you wanna talk to someone."

"I'm comin' over."

"You can't cuz they got that yellow tape everywhere."

"Marcel?"

"What?"

"Where's Dante?"

"Gone. He was gone b'fore the police came."

"Marcel? You okay, little dude?"

"Yeah, but Latrice and my mama ain't. I gotta go now becuz my auntie gotta use the phone. Bye."

"Bye, little dude," I said.

I threw the phone across the room. It broke into pieces. My moms knocked on my door.

"Jamal?"

I couldn't answer.

She turned the doorknob and came in.

"What's goin' on?" she said.

I stared at the wall.

She sat down beside me. "Jamal?"

I hung my head and cried.

Eddie

My father had put my graduation portrait up in his market. *Muy bonito,* all the women told him. *Muy bonito.* He was full of pride and my mother seemed happy again. I felt like everything was going to be okay.

I got off the bus that Monday morning and walked up the front steps of school. People were standing around like football players in a huddle, talking in whispers.

I approached a small group. "What's up with everyone?"

"Emako," a girl named Mona replied.

"What?"

"Didn't you hear?" another girl asked.

"It was on the news," said another.

"A drive-by," Mona added.

"She's dead," someone said softly.

I dropped my backpack.

"Monterey was with her, but she's all right."

I couldn't speak.

"You a'ight, Eddie?" Darryl from chorus asked.

I slumped against the lockers. "But . . ." I slid to the floor and pulled my knees up to my chest.

"You okay?" Darryl asked again.

I jumped up, picked up my backpack, and ran outside. The next thing I remember, I was home.

I called Monterey. Her father answered the phone. "Hello?"

"Hi . . . this is Eddie."

"Hi, Eddie. Monterey's asleep, finally. I'll tell her you called."

"Is she okay?" I asked.

"Hard to tell right now," he replied.

"Tell her I called."

"I said I would."

"Okay . . . good-bye," I said.

"Good-bye."

This had to be a dream.

Savannah

On Monday, I was late as usual and I had to go to the office to get a tardy slip so that I could get into first period. The people in the office looked like someone had sucked the life out of them, but I just figured it was because it was Monday. I got my tardy slip and went to class. Everyone looked sad, like maybe the teacher had just announced a pop quiz or something.

Anyway, I handed the teacher my tardy slip and took my seat at the back of the classroom.

No one was talking.

I said to this girl named Marcella who sits in front of me, "Did someone die or something?" and I started to laugh.

The whole class must have heard me, because they all turned around and the teacher called me up to the front of the classroom and told me that this was not the time for jokes. Then she told us to open our books, turn to chapter five, and read silently.

I went back to my seat. Marcella turned around and asked me, "Didn't you hear the announcement?"

"I was late," I replied.

"Emako," she said.

"Yeah, what about her?"

"She's dead."

"What?"

"She got shot."

"Where?"

"In front of her house."

"You lyin'."

"Shhh," the teacher said from the front of the class.

I opened my book and stared at the pages. I couldn't read. The words looked like a foreign language. This can't be real, I thought. I didn't want her to die.

Monterey

We followed the white hearse and limousine to the grave-yard. I looked back and saw the endless line of cars with their headlights on, crawling slowly through the streets like a snake with a hundred eyes.

At the cemetery a crowd had gathered around Verna, who was sitting in one of the white folding chairs between Latrice and Marcel.

I felt a breeze and looked up. A cloud sat in front of the sun like a see-through curtain, but the air still tasted hot.

I thought about Emako's body in her pretty box, putting her in the ground, the last good-bye.

A car outside the cemetery backfired and the crowd turned, startled. I began to shake. Daddy put his arm in mine. Mama took my hand and held it. I leaned into her and put my head on her shoulder. My mama, she was cool and sweet like ice cream.

The people from the funeral home stood around, ushering, directing the show. It was Emako's final performance.

I wiped tears from my face.

The preacher approached Verna and held her hands. Then he turned to the head of the casket and began to speak. His words floated through the air. "Let us pray. Heavenly Father, we say to You, this child is gone, but she will never be forgotten. This child is gone before she ever got to fly. This child is gone and we pray that no more will be lost in this way. And let us not be filled with hatred, but let us rest with the knowledge that everything in the dark will be brought into the light. In the name and by the power of Jesus Christ, we pray. Amen."

The crowd replied, "Amen."

A woman wearing a royal blue hat began to sing "Go Tell It on the Mountain." She looked like she weighed 300 pounds and sweat covered her face and poured down to her neck like a stream.

When she finished, the preacher led us in another prayer and Emako's mother doubled over, bent in half, sobbing. Latrice and Marcel pulled her to her feet and the pretty pink casket was lowered into the ground.

The preacher whispered, "Ashes to ashes, dust to dust."

Jamal

Eddie asked me for a ride to the cemetery. I wanted to be alone, but I said yes because we were cool.

We followed the trail of cars out of the parking lot, and a fat brother on a motorcycle waved us through a red light. I wondered how a fat man rode a motorcycle. I pictured him tipping over like Humpty Dumpty and falling off the wall. My mind was playing tricks on me.

The line of cars inched its way slowly through the cemetery. Eddie sat there, looking out the window. In twenty minutes not a single word passed between us. I was glad. I didn't feel like talking. I parked the car and we got out. I had forgotten my sunglasses and the smog and sun burned my eyes.

Emako's mother was sitting, and someone was standing over her with an umbrella to protect her from the heat. There were people all around her, but she looked alone and lonely. I walked over to her and reached for her hand. She put her wet tissue in her lap.

She pulled me in close and whispered, "She was a good girl, wasn't she?" She looked into my eyes.

"She was," I replied.

She squeezed my hand and I shivered.

The people from the mortuary were acting like they cared, but I thought that for them it was just another day, just another body being put in the ground.

I walked away from the crowd to be by myself.

I waited under a tree, watching from a distance, and when the casket was in the ground, I went over to this church lady who was handing out white roses and took one.

I tossed the rose in the grave and whispered good-bye.

Marcel came over beside me. "Hey, little dude," I said, rubbing the top of his head.

"Hey, Jamal."

"How you doin', Marcel?" I asked.

"I'm scared."

"Of what?"

"To go back to our house. Everyone keeps saying they gonna come back looking for Dante. So me and Latrice are goin' to live in San Diego with my auntie."

"For how long?"

"Forever. Mama's gonna sell the house and move down there too. She said we gotta get away."

I put my hand on his shoulder. "Stay outta trouble, little dude."

"I will," he said.

Eddie

While Jamal drove, I took in the panoramic view of the skyline. Palm trees basked in the sun against a background of blue. Suddenly, I felt ashamed for admiring the beauty of this world.

I wanted to tell Jamal that this was all just a crazy dream. *Muy loco.* I wanted to tell him that it was okay to wake up now. Emako was going to open her eyes and arise from the coffin the way a vampire awakens after dark.

The gates of the cemetery were painted white and I thought about how, when I was a little kid, my mother told me that Saint Peter was always standing at the gates of heaven. I asked her, When did God let him go to sleep, but she said that in heaven no one has to sleep. I always wondered how she knew that.

I hiked up the hill to where the casket was waiting like a wrapped gift to God, pink with white roses, and wandered through the crowd.

A woman from the mortuary was wearing white gloves and I wondered why. Maybe it was to keep death from touching her. It had to get to you.

I found Monterey and touched her on the shoulder and I hugged her for a long time. It felt good to have my arms around her.

I took a deep breath and the tears finally came.

Savannah

I checked my watch as I left the church. It was almost 12:00 and my mother was late. I found a place in the shade and called her on my cell phone.

"What is it, Savannah?" she asked.

"You're late and it's hot."

"I'm still at the salon. Marquis decided to give me blond highlights."

"Bonjour, Savannah," Marquis spoke into the phone. "Your mother looks delicious."

"Yeah, *bonjour,*" I replied.

"I'm on my way out the door," my mother said.

"Could you hurry up?" I said, and ended the call.

I looked around. The parking lot was starting to empty.

A black man with bloodshot eyes stumbled up to me. His dreads were matted and he was wearing dirty clothes. He spoke softly. "Hey, young sister. Gotta few dollars for a hungry brother?"

I backed up and took ten dollars out of my purse.

"Thank you," he said, taking the money. Seeing it was a ten, he said, "God bless you."

"You're welcome," I replied.

"You take care," he added, and walked away without looking back.

I checked my watch again and sat down on the church steps. Car after car turned the corner and drove off. They all had orange funeral stickers printed with black letters that spelled *funeral*. I wondered why the word *funeral* started with *fun*. There was nothing fun about it.

■ ■ ■

My mother finally rolled up to the church. "Do you want to go to the cemetery?" she asked.

"No, I hate cemeteries."

"Do you want to go shopping?"

I stared at her like she was crazy.

"Well?"

"Just take me home."

As we headed toward the freeway, she started to talk. "Urban blight and South Central. They should be synonyms What these people need are jobs, jobs and education."

I wanted to scream, Shut up!

"We could stop and have lunch?"

"I'm not hungry," I replied.

When we got home, I went outside to the patio. I thought about getting in the pool, but it started to rain, so I went inside and got in bed. As soon as I closed my eyes, the phone rang.

"Was Jamal there?" Gina asked.

"Of course Jamal was there," I replied.

"Did she look good?"

"Even I cannot believe you would ask me a question like that, but, yes, she looked good," I answered. "I'm tired, Gina. Call me back later," I said, and hung up the phone.

I pulled the covers over my head, trying hard to go to sleep.

■ ■ ■

The sound of the rain on the roof woke me up. The day had turned dark. Lillie was scratching at my door and I crawled out from under the covers and let her in. She was shaking like a leaf. I got back in bed and put her under the covers with me. Thunder shook the house and a flash of lightning lit up the patio.

I thought about what it felt like to have a bullet in your chest. I wondered how scared she must have been and I felt real bad.

Why is it when someone looks good and has talent and

115

the future seems to belong to her, that people like me give her a hard time, like it's her fault she was born lucky? And how could someone's life be over just like that? Just like that. So now I'm left to deal with all the lies and trash I threw her way. I knew that some people deserved to go to hell, but I didn't want to be one of them.

My mother knocked on the door. I figured she was just looking for Lillie. "She's in here," I said.

My mother sat down beside me on the bed.

"You want to talk?"

I couldn't believe my ears. "Yeah, I do."

"She was nice, this girl?"

"Real nice."

Jamal

It had started to rain and people rushed to their cars. I looked around for Eddie. He was walking down the hill and I ran after him.

"Eddie?" I said, catching him.

"What?"

"Where you goin'?"

"Home," he replied.

"I'll give you a ride. C'mon."

"It's a long drive."

"Ain't nuthin'."

We drove out the gates of the cemetery onto the slick streets. My shirt was wet and I shivered.

"I still can't believe this," I said. "I keep thinking it's all a dream."

"Me too," Eddie replied.

"When I woke up this morning, I thought the dream was over and everything was gonna be the way it was. You know, like I'm gonna call her and she's gonna pick up the phone and say, 'Hey.'"

"I know."

"And I keep askin' myself why. I mean, why her? She never hurt anyone."

"I don't know, dude." He paused. "Make a left at the corner."

I turned left and kept talking. "I mean, I thought we were gonna get serious . . . real serious."

Eddie kept quiet, like a head doctor. Finally Eddie spoke. "If her brother hadn't got out, she'd still be alive."

"Yeah, that mutha. It's like he brought death to her door."

"You could get on the freeway up here at the on-ramp. It's quicker."

"I'll take the streets." The truth was, I needed to talk.

"She was real nice," Eddie said.

The windshield wipers went back and forth. "She was . . ."—I hesitated for a moment—"I hate to admit it, but at first I was just runnin' my game, treatin' her like she was just another honey, you know, tryin' to be a player, and then all of a sudden I started lovin' her. Now it feels like someone took a bat to my heart and beat the hell out of it."

"Yeah . . . she was too sweet," Eddie said.

"You goin' to school tomorrow?"

"Yeah, I have a test."

We drove the rest of the way to Eddie's house in silence. I pulled up in front of his door and he got out.

"Later, dawg," I said.

"Yeah, later," Eddie replied.

I drove off and looked in the rearview mirror. Eddie was standing in the rain, getting drenched.

I put in the Aaliyah CD she liked, and headed back to the cemetery. I wanted to be alone with her one more time.

When I got there, everyone was gone and they had already filled up the grave with dirt.

I sat down on the wet grass, crossed my legs, and cried.

Eddie

I stood in the rain, watching Jamal turn the corner. Then I went around to the side of the house. As usual, the door was unlocked.

"Hey, Eddie," my sister said from her room as I passed by.

"You know you should keep the door locked," I said.

Suddenly, I heard a loud noise and jumped. "What was that?" I said.

"I dropped the remote control," Hortensia replied.

"Oh." Now, every time I heard a loud noise, I got nervous.

As I changed into dry clothes, I wondered if I would make it. If they got Emako, then maybe they would get me too. They could keep my brother, Tomas, incarcerated forever as far as I was concerned. I didn't want him bringing the angel of death to our door. I knew now that innocence didn't mean anything.

Hortensia knocked on my door.

"It's open," I said.

She came into my room. "Were there a lot of people there?" she asked.

"The church was full," I said.

"Did you go to the cemetery?"

"Yeah."

"Sorry," she said.

"About what?"

"About your friend."

I looked at my pretty baby sister and wondered what was going to happen to her when I was gone.

I was going to make my mother and father promise not to ever let Tomas come back and call this home.

I was going to make my mother swear before Jesus.

I pulled out my wallet and looked at the paper with Monterey's number and the smiley face. Love.

Arizona isn't that far away, I thought.

Monterey

The crowd began to scatter.

I went over to where Verna was standing and she took my hand in hers. "She was my sweet girl. Since she was little, she was just a little sweet thing. Always bringing me something, sometimes just a little flower she'd picked from someone's yard. She'd hand it to me after I'd dragged in from work and it made me smile. It ain't right that she died that way."

"I'm sorry, Verna," I said.

"Y'all comin' to the house?" she asked. "We gotta mountain of food."

I hesitated. "I can't." I remembered the sound of the bullets. "I can't," I repeated.

"I know," was all she said.

She let go of my hand and I went back to my mama and daddy. The rain was falling harder and my clothes were getting wet.

By the time we got in the car, the wind had started to blow and it felt like God was mad. Lightning punched through the clouds.

"You need to get out of those wet things soon as we get into the house," Mama said. "You still have that blanket in the truck, Roman?"

"Yes."

Mama got out of the ██████████████████████ flannel blanket out of the trun████████████████████████with them to baseball games in ██████ ████ ███ ████ the backseat door and put it around my shoulders.

"I can do it myself! I'm not a baby anymore!" I pushed away my mother's hands. "Stop treating me like I'm a baby!"

Mama was silent.

Then Daddy turned around. "She's right. She's not a child anymore, DeeDee."

"Yeah," I replied.

"But, Monterey, one thing," Daddy added.

"What?"

"Put your seat belt on."

I fastened my seat belt as Daddy drove through the cemetery toward the gates. I looked at row after row of

WHO WAS
Emako Blue?

She was beautiful and good-hearted. She was Monterey's best friend. She was the only girl Jamal cared about, the one who saw through his player act. She was the one who understood the burden of Eddie's family. She was the best singer anyone had ever heard, with a voice like vanilla incense, smoky and sweet. She was Savannah's rival, the one who wouldn't play by the rules. She was destined for greatness, already plucked from South Central Los Angeles by the record producers. She was only fifteen when she died.

Emako Blue was supposed to be a star. But life can change in a flash.

"This short, succinct, and poignant story of friendship, family, and overwhelming sadness will leave some readers in tears."
—*SLJ*

An ALA Quick Pick Top Ten Title
A New York Public Library Book for the Teen Age

Cover art and design by Kristina ewell

speak
U.S.A. $5.99 CAN. $8.50
VISIT US AT
www.penguin.com/teens

ISBN 0-14-240418-7

50599> EAN

9 780142 404188

"I know," was all she said.

She let go of my hand and I went back to my mama and daddy. The rain was falling harder and my clothes were getting wet.

By the time we got in the car, the wind had started to blow and it felt like God was mad. Lightning punched through the clouds.

"You need to get out of those wet things soon as we get into the house," Mama said. "You still have that blanket in the truck, Roman?"

"Yes."

Mama got out of the ⬛⬛⬛⬛⬛⬛⬛⬛⬛⬛⬛⬛⬛⬛⬛⬛ nel blanket out of the trun⬛⬛⬛⬛⬛⬛⬛⬛⬛⬛⬛⬛⬛ with them to baseball games in ca⬛⬛⬛ g⬛⬛⬛⬛⬛⬛⬛ the backseat door and put it around my shoulders.

"I can do it myself! I'm not a baby anymore!" I pushed away my mother's hands. "Stop treating me like I'm a baby!"

Mama was silent.

Then Daddy turned around. "She's right. She's not a child anymore, DeeDee."

"Yeah," I replied.

"But, Monterey, one thing," Daddy added.

"What?"

"Put your seat belt on."

I fastened my seat belt as Daddy drove through the cemetery toward the gates. I looked at row after row of graves and thought I didn't want Emako to be gone. I wanted her to come back and finish growing up with me and I wanted to hear her say, "Hey, Monterey," again and I wanted her to diss me and smile and I wanted her to be rich and famous and I wanted to tell her that she had the most beautiful awesome voice I'd ever heard. It wasn't supposed to be this way.

■ ■ ■

My friend, Emako Blue, was supposed to be a star.

BRENDA WOODS's debut novel, *The Red Rose Box*, won a Coretta Scott King Honor and was a finalist for the PEN Center USA's 2003 Literary Award. It also received the 2003 Judy Lopez Memorial Award for Children's Literature presented by the Women's National Book Association. A longtime resident of Los Angeles, she is currently working on her third novel.

WHO WAS

Emako Blue?

She was beautiful and good-hearted. She was Monterey's best friend. She was the only girl Jamal cared about, the one who saw through his player act. She was the one who understood the burden of Eddie's family. She was the best singer anyone had ever heard, with a voice like vanilla incense, smoky and sweet. She was Savannah's rival, the one who wouldn't play by the rules. She was destined for greatness, already plucked from South Central Los Angeles by the record producers. She was only fifteen when she died.

Emako Blue was supposed to be a star. But life can change in a flash.

"This short, succinct, and poignant story of friendship, family, and overwhelming sadness will leave some readers in tears."

—*SLJ*

An ALA Quick Pick Top Ten Title
A New York Public Library Book for the Teen Age

Cover art and design by Kristina Duewell

ISBN 0-14-240418-7

9 780142 404188

50599>

EAN